Baby, It's Cold Outside

Contemporary Romance

Baby, It's Cold Outside

A Wintertime Treasury for Lovers

E. Ayers

A Cowboy's Holiday

Christmas at Mariner's Cove

The Charity Auction

Indie Artist Press
Eagle Mountain, Utah

Contemporary Romance:
Baby, It's Cold Outside-
A Wintertime Treasury for Lovers
by E. Ayers
Published by Indie Artist Press
Eagle Mountain, Utah
www.indieartistpress.com
First Print Edition
copyright © 2013-2015
All rights reserved.
ISBN-13: 978-1-62522-076-9
December 2015

To George, who believed in me.

A Cowboy's Holiday

*

*H*annah Smith was sitting by a window. She seemed to be staring into nothingness. Her dark brown hair was pulled into a large clip and some of it had escaped the plastic jaws and now tumbled down her back.

Jeremy McCullough walked over, lightly tugged on her wayward lock of hair and put his cup of coffee on her table as he slid onto the seat across from her. "Hi. Penny for your thoughts."

She looked at him and smiled. "Hi. Not thinking about much of anything. Are you going home for the holidays?"

"Yeah. Three days of driving. I tried doing it in two and almost fell asleep behind the wheel. With the snow that is predicted, it might take me more than three."

"You're lucky. You get to go home."

"You're not going home?"

She shook her head. "Can't afford it. My mom is military and my dad and siblings went with her. She's not even in this country. She's in Japan."

"What are you going to do?"

"Same thing as last Christmas. Stay here." Her smile looked forced. "I was hoping you'd be here, too. Keep each other company and all that."

This is worth a try and it just might be my lucky break. "Why don't you come with me? Ever been to Wyoming?"

"I've been to a lot of places growing up, but never to Wyoming." She grimaced. "But I can't just go home with you. It's not as though you live an hour away."

"I don't morph at night into a crazed animal with claws, nor am I an axe murderer. I promise I'm a gentleman, and my family will welcome you with open arms." He pulled his phone from his pocket. "Listen."

He touched the screen and the phone began to ring. "Hi, Grandma. May I bring a filly home with me? She doesn't have any place to go for Christmas."

"Of course, you may. Is there anything more to this story that you'd like to tell me?"

He could hear the smile in his grandmother's words. "No. She's just a fellow student. But I don't want her staying here on campus alone over the holiday."

"But if she's more than just a friend…"

"Grandma, I promise, she's just a friend and would appreciate the guest room."

"Are you sure? You're a grown man. No one is going to say anything if you want her in your room."

He could feel the heat headed for his cheeks, and prayed it wouldn't show as he winked at Hannah. "Really, Grandma. She's just a friend. We've taken classes together, and we often run into each other on campus."

Hannah put her hand on her forehead as her cheeks flushed, and she lowered her gaze to her almost empty coffee cup.

"Well, of course, she's welcome to come. It's nothing for me to set an extra plate. Besides it *is* Christmas. You two talk it over, and let me know when you are on the road."

"I will, Grandma. Thanks." He disconnected the call and grinned at Hannah. "See, it was that easy.

You're coming home with me."

"But I don't have a bunch of extra money to pay for hotel rooms between there and here."

"Don't worry about any expenses. I can cover everything."

"Professor Hadley invited me to have Christmas dinner with her family. It's not that I won't have any place to go. She's very nice, and often has students over who are stuck here."

"You're coming with me."

"But I–"

"Hannah, you're coming with me... as a friend... to my family's ranch. I promise I'm a total gentleman."

Hannah giggled. "You never struck me as being anything else."

He rolled his palms so they faced up. "I'm a normal male, but my parents raised me to at least act like a decent one. Just wear *really* ugly pajamas, because I don't need any temptation."

She laughed. "Does that mean you like me?"

"Why wouldn't I? Let's grab some pizza. I want to get some sleep tonight. I like getting on the road early."

"Are you asking me out on a date?"

"Call it whatever you want. I'll call it pizza with a friend." He swigged down the last of his coffee. "If we go now, it'll be quieter. I think there are some holiday parties planned for tonight, and I'd like to be asleep before that happens."

She pushed her chair back. "I'm fine with that."

꙳

At five o'clock in the morning, Hannah, still bleary-eyed, dragged her suitcase out of her apartment and into the parking lot where Jeremy greeted her.

"Not much of a morning person?"

She knitted her eyebrows together and watched as he stowed her bag in the cab of his pickup truck. "It's not morning. The sun isn't up."

"What time did you go to bed?"

"Midnight. I had to do laundry so I had something to pack."

He laughed and held the passenger door for her. "You can go back to sleep."

"I should have brought my pillow."

"Well, go get it."

She turned and went back into the building. *What am I doing up? What am I thinking? I'm not.* On the third floor, she unlocked her apartment door and grabbed her fuzzy throw and the pillow from her bed.

Great. I'm taking my blankie and my pillow. He's going to think I've lost my mind.

She returned to his truck, and he held the door for her.

"There's coffee for you in the cup holder."

How can he be so awake? She fastened her seatbelt and sipped the coffee. It was perfect. "How did you know what I like in my coffee?"

"Do you realize how many times I've watched you fix your cup?"

Warmth emanated from the seat where she sat. She looked around the cab, and it looked like a luxury car complete with a large computer screen in the dash.

He was saying something about beating the morning traffic on the interstate, but she tucked her fuzzy throw around her legs, put her head on the pillow, and closed her eyes.

She awakened to discover they were driving through flurries. They had lunch from a fast food drive-thru, but when they stopped for dinner, they ate at a truck stop. About eight thirty, they pulled into a small motel, and Jeremy got a room for them. Suddenly the pleasant day they had spent together dissolved when she realized he'd only reserved a single room with two beds.

Her insides clenched. She'd never spent a night with a man. Now she was miles from school with almost no money, and she was with Jeremy McCullough, one of the hottest, smartest guys at school. Probably every female in the veterinary school would have killed to be alone in a motel room with him. *So why am I feeling like a trapped animal?*

"Pick a bed." He looked around. "Don't bother. I'm taking the one closest to the door. That one is yours."

"Why do you say that?"

"Protection. A man sleeps closest to the door in case there's an intruder or something."

She raised her eyebrows and looked at him.

He checked the room and the bathroom. "All's well. Why don't you use the bathroom first to do whatever, such as put on *really* ugly pajamas, and then I will."

"I don't think I own ugly pajamas."

He chuckled. "Neither do I."

She watched him blow a long breath between pursed lips as he sat on the edge of the bed and grabbed the remote. Something inside told her he was feeling just as awkward about the situation.

The TV clicked on and he flipped through a few channels.

She took her nightshirt, flannel sleeping pants, and a bag of toiletries into the bathroom with her. Quickly, she showered and brushed her teeth. Dressed in her night things, she returned to the room. He had turned down her bed for her. The TV was off, and he was using his computer tablet.

"There's WIFI here." He barely looked at her.

He had changed from his jeans into some pajama bottoms and only wore a short-sleeved T-shirt. Every muscle on him showed. *Omigod, he's sexy.* She slipped between the cold sheets. *Now what? Do I just say goodnight?*

✳

Without moving his head, Jeremy glanced up and inhaled. Every curve on Hannah showed under her long-sleeved knit shirt. *Don't think about it.*

He heard her climb into her bed, and knew he was going to be in for a rough night. "I'll take my shower in the morning. It helps me wake up."

"Whatever."

He used the small bathroom and realized it smelled of her feminine presence, a little like roses and herbs. *Sleep. I need sleep. Don't think about it.*

A few minutes later, he returned to the main room. She was curled on her side and he assumed she was asleep, until he caught her watching him. He set the alarm on his phone and glanced at her. She quickly closed her eyes. "I know you're awake. I want to be on the road at five. What time do you want me to wake you?"

She rolled away from him. "Four thirty?"

"That'll work."

It seemed as though sleep would never come. He tossed and turned, and when he couldn't stand it any longer, he got up and went into the bathroom. It didn't help that he was certain that she wasn't sleeping either. When he returned, he quietly opened the door to the parking lot and looked out. Crispy cold air instantly cooled him. He watched big flakes of snow softly floating downward. Several inches of snow coated his truck. According to the weather forecast, they were headed into a major storm. He needed some solid sleep.

When the alarm sounded, he jumped up. He peeked through the curtains that covered a large windowpane, and the snow was coming down hard. The sooner they were on their way, the safer they'd be.

He made a pot of coffee in the motel's little four-cup pot in their room and then jumped into the shower. Now he kicked himself over his sexual attraction to Hannah that had kept him awake. Instead of getting a full eight hours of sleep, he remembered seeing eleven forty-three on his phone. *Less than four hours.* She could sleep in the truck, but he had to drive. At a little after four, he woke her and handed her a paper cup of coffee. "We're going to get out of here while we can still get back on the highway."

She nodded and ran to the bathroom.

As she closed the door, he called, "Don't take too long. I'm giving you fifteen minutes to get ready."

He grabbed a few granola bars from the vending machine at the motel and then loaded their things into the cab. He was glad he'd gassed up before they had pulled in last night. The plows were out and the road had been treated, but the snow was falling faster than the plows could clear it.

He tried to stay relaxed and not tense up as he drove, but he couldn't make any time. The road was nothing more than tire tracks from the other vehicles in front of him. By three o'clock in the afternoon, he pulled into a truck stop and inquired about a room. "I need two beds."

"This isn't the Hilton; it's a truck stop. Only one

I've got left is a king."

Another man walked into the tiny office. "I need a room."

"I've got one left. If he doesn't want it, it's yours."

Panic seized Jeremy. He was tired and beat. As far as he was concerned, he and Hannah could sleep in shifts. He just knew it was no longer safe for him to keep going. "I'm taking it."

He filled out the form, swiped his credit card through the card reader, and signed his name on the electronic pad. *She's not going to be happy.*

✻

Hannah looked at the lone bed and wasn't certain if she wanted to kill Jeremy or cry.

"If you don't want to sleep with me, that's fine, but I've got to get a few hours." He pulled off his boots, jeans, and a shirt, revealing a set of long johns. Three minutes later, he was sound asleep.

She paced around the room and stared at him. Other girls would have been green with envy over the opportunity to spend the night with Jeremy, and many she knew spent nights with their boyfriends. But she wasn't one of them.

Having grown up in southern ports, driving in blinding snow had scared her. Twice Jeremy managed to avoid cars spinning out of control, and the number of vehicles that littered the roads was unreal. She was probably just as tired and worn out from being tense.

A little after six, she left a note in the room and trudged her way through the snow to the truck stop's restaurant and ordered dinner-to-go for both of them.

As she opened the motel room's door, she called, "Hey, Jeremy. I bought some food for us. Wake up and eat."

He grabbed the food, downed it, and returned to bed without saying more than a few sentences. By seven thirty that evening, his truck was nothing more than a white blob in the parking lot. By nine, she decided she was too tired and bored to do anything but sleep.

Still in her jeans, she tentatively pulled down the covers on her side of the bed and gingerly climbed in. She listened to the gentle rhythmic sounds of him breathing. Her body warmed from the realization of his proximity. *What am I doing here?*

She had fallen in love with him the first day he walked into the classroom. He had an earthy look to him, and his cowboy getups were real, not that of a city boy trying to look like one. Jeremy was one.

Cornell was probably the most elite of all the veterinary schools in America, so to some extent she understood how a rancher's son would come east to study. But it wasn't until they had a few classes together that she realized how intelligent he was. There wasn't a student there that wasn't topnotch, but Jeremy had them all beat. He also had a big smile and easy way about him, but she never heard anything about him partying. He had hooked up with another female student, but he never acted like they were a couple. Although Jennifer Deleon made it quite clear that Jeremy belonged to her. Hannah wondered what the relationship really was.

Hannah had just about killed herself to make certain she ran into him as often as possible at the coffee shop or in the cafeteria. He'd sit beside her and even put his arm across the back of her chair. She'd managed to be his lab partner a few times, and he always treated her like she was his sister. Now he slept inches from her.

She woke once and realized she was tucked against his body and his arm held her in a protective embrace. Afraid to move, she was aware of the steady rise and fall of his chest against her back.

Truck noise outside awakened her and this time she was curled to his chest. Her attempt to roll away was thwarted as his arm tightened and held her close. He mumbled something that sounded like don't go.

When his alarm went off, he sprang from the bed and dashed into the bathroom. He returned, grabbed a few things from his duffle bag, and the next thing she heard was water running.

"Hey sleepyhead, wake up. There's a ton of snow, but it's stopped falling."

She dragged herself from the bed and peered out the window. Everything was buried in snow, but not a flake could be seen in the tall lights of the parking lot.

"While you get ready, I'm going to see if I can shovel us out."

"You're joking."

"Nope." He strode over to her and planted a kiss on her cheek. "Wish me luck. Let's see if we can get out of here. If not, we'll just have to get back in bed so you can put your head on my chest. That felt wonderful."

Heat flew to her cheeks and she discovered the sensation of butterflies flitting in her abdomen.

He grinned and ran his fingers through her hair. "That's what I call good sleeping."

She watched him put on his coat and go outside,

but the butterflies inside her wouldn't settle down.

✳

Shoveling snow took Jeremy's mind off of Hannah in a sexual context. He wouldn't have said there was anything particularly striking about Hannah other than her rich brown hair that she usually attempted to confine in some way or another, but it always escaped. Yet she was easy on the eyes – real easy and intelligent with lots of common sense. He also knew she didn't date anyone.

She buried her nose in her books and was extremely diligent. Plus she wasn't squeamish and tackled hard work head on. He could see himself with someone like her. She'd blend in with his family.

Several of his female classmates were daughters of farmers and a few were horse enthusiasts, but Hannah was neither. From the things she had said, she was looking more towards the laboratory end of veterinary science. But unlike the others, she had a strong work ethic and had no problems with cattle.

The only vet he'd ever known had been Doc Medino. The man had an office in Creed's Crossing, but ran a mobile practice because no one put a sick steer in a trailer and took them to an office.

And having grown up on a ranch, Jeremy had learned to do things such as deliver a foal or calf. He probably was eight years old when his pony ran into problems foaling. His grandfather talked him through the steps to help her. That incident cemented Jeremy's desire to become a veterinarian. Then as a teen, he spent summers volunteering with Doc Medino.

But Hannah seemed almost aloof until this trip. He was certain that asking her to come with him was the best move he could have ever made. It wasn't from lack of trying, but it seemed the most he ever could do was catch her in the library, at the coffee shop, or maybe in the cafeteria. But realizing she was in his arms as he slept did something to him. He didn't deny his sexual attraction to a pretty female, but Hannah was more than a pretty female. He liked her. He enjoyed her friendship, and her quiet mannerisms. Having her on this trip had changed something inside of him – it reinforced his feelings towards her. It was as though she was his woman and he had to protect her.

The truck stop had a convenience store and, when he finished shoveling, he went there and loaded up on foods that would keep. As he wandered the aisles of the small store, he pulled his phone from his pocket and called home. "Hey, Derrick, what are you doing up at this hour?"

"Drinking coffee. We're buried in snow here, but we didn't get it like parts of South Dakota and Iowa. They are getting slammed. Are you trying to drive home through this?"

"Yeah. It stopped snowing. Maybe I can make up for lost time."

"Better check the road conditions. It stopped here for about eight hours, and it's coming down like crazy again. Heard you got a filly."

Jeremy chuckled. "Yeah. Can I ask you something?"

"Go ahead."

"Was there a time when you held Chessie in your arms and knew that she was the one?"

"Oh yeah. She just fit my body – as though we were meant to be together."

"I'm feeling that way, and I've never had her in a good arm lock or played kissy-face."

"Watch your step."

"I will. Tell Mom, when I get close, I'll call, but right now, I don't know when that will be. We must have had over a foot of snow in less than twelve hours. I got a room about three o'clock yesterday afternoon. I could barely see the taillights of the vehicle in front of me. I'm hoping I'll make better time today."

"Good luck with that. Be safe, and be real careful if you want her."

"I will be."

Jeremy paid for the basketful of food he'd picked up at the convenience store and headed back to the motel room. He tossed most of his food purchases in the truck. Traveling with certain supplies in the winter were required, but those ready to eat meals his dad had stored in the emergency kit were lousy.

"Omigod, you're here! I didn't know what happened to you."

He motioned with his thumb towards the truck. "I picked up some peanuts and stuff for us. Apparently we're in for more bad weather. I thought maybe we had cleared it. Guess not. There's more snow ahead of us. We'll grab some food in the café before we leave. Hope you're hungry."

Once they were on the road, Jeremy sighed with relief. The interstate was plowed and they made reasonable time. But by mid afternoon, the weather had turned once again into blinding whiteness.

According to the GPS, there was another truck stop a few miles ahead. He tried to follow the rear lights of a tractor-trailer, but the truck ground to a halt and the trailer fell onto its side.

"Oh no-o-o," Jeremy hissed and slammed his fist on the steering wheel. He had followed the truck off the road. At least he hadn't put the ranch's pickup in a ditch, but he had no idea where the road was. "Guess we're stuck here until help arrives."

The trucker got out and looked around. Jeremy knew the man was okay. But that wasn't helping Jeremy's mood. Snow kept coming and Jeremy got out several times and cleared the snow from the vehicle and from around the exhaust pipes.

There were a handful of odd supplies in the locked toolbox that went from one side of the truck's bed to the other side. He found an orange traffic cone with a battery operated flasher and placed it on the corner edge of the truck's bed. He prayed that no one would plow into him.

He tried his phone and it was dead. He had plenty of charge, but no signal. Hannah didn't have a signal either. "Either there's damage to the nearest tower, or we're in a dead zone. I'm willing to bet, in this storm, it's tower damage."

"Now what?" Hannah asked with more than a hint of concern in her voice.

"We wait. We're going to hope we see a snow plow

and I can shovel us from here to the road."

Hannah's eyes filled with tears, but she tried to hide them. They ate some peanuts and drank the semi-frozen individual-sized chocolate milk jugs that Jeremy had placed in the toolbox. He brought the other food items he'd stowed there into the cab.

Every so often he'd clear snow and turn the engine on long enough to heat the cab. He grabbed some jeans from his duffle and tried to create a soft bridge between the two seats so that Hanna could sit closer to him. She was shivering even when he wasn't.

"What are you wearing under your jeans?"

She looked at him. "Underwear."

"No long johns?"

"Don't own any."

He reached in his bag and pulled out a pair. "For you. Put them on. I don't want you dying of hypothermia from this. I'll turn my back."

She seemed to hesitate and then he heard her slipping off her jeans and wiggling in the seat.

"Okay. I'm dressed again, but now I've got to pee."

He looked at her and laughed. "Open your door and step out."

"What?"

"Do you see a bathroom nearby? You take that side and I'll take this one. There's something about the power of suggestion."

They both laughed.

They ate potato chips and chocolate. They ate some beef jerky and some cheese and crackers.

"I'm sure it's rare, but I've heard of people being stuck for days. We'd better be careful of what we eat just in case. I'm scared, Jeremy. You hear about people who get stranded like this and die."

"We'll be fine. I'm not happy about this, but I'm not scared. I know what I can do. Just keep watching for any lights." He held out his arms to Hannah and she curled up against him. He tossed the old wool blanket he had over them and then hers over that. "I'm glad you brought your blanket. It's extra warmth."

She slept and he watched for any signs of another vehicle. It was well after dark when he spotted yellow flashing lights approaching from behind his pickup truck. "Wake up. I think we have a snow plow!"

He got out and took a flare gun with him. As the light approached, he fired it. The plow stopped.

"You okay?" the driver shouted.

"Freezing cold, but okay. Let me follow you! That tractor-trailer is in big trouble, but the driver appears to be okay."

Jeremy grabbed the shovel and cleared enough to

fall in behind the plow. The man radioed the big truck's plight to the state police, but the trucker had no desire to leave his rig.

An hour later, Jeremy pulled into another truck stop. Jeremy gassed up his truck, but there was no place to sleep. The convenience store clerk said there was a motel in town and called to check on accommodations. Jeremy said he'd take whatever they had.

The little town's roads weren't exactly in good shape but he made it. His cell phone still didn't work. He looked at the time and knew the entire family would be asleep. He'd call home in the morning.

Even if the weather had been good, he would have one hard day ahead of him, but with all the snow, he figured at least sixteen hours of driving. In the little motel, they watched the weather report on the TV. State police were begging people to stay off the roads and the interstate was officially closed. And after running off the road, he didn't want to chance a secondary road. They'd stay where they were.

He looked around the tiny room and laughed. "Remind me never to stay here again. What is this, a no-tell motel?"

Hannah giggled. "The sheets look clean."

"At least, it's warm."

Hannah was peeling off the layers of clothes that she had pulled on while they were trapped.

"Um, before you go any further..." He strode to where she was standing and played with a strand of her hair that had slipped from the confines of a large clip. "It's only fair to tell you..."

*

Hannah looked at him and he grinned as he placed his hands on her shoulders. His pretty hazel-green eyes stared back into hers. He was the most confident man she'd ever known. And she couldn't imagine spending three grueling days with anyone other than him.

"I wanted to tell you that I didn't expect this kind of weather. I thought we'd drive through it and that would be the end of it. If I had known, I would have postponed this trip. But part of me is thrilled to have spent this much time with you." He kissed her cheek. "I can't imagine anyone else at my side, or when I've enjoyed being with anyone as much."

She scrunched up her nose. "Are you trying to tell me something?"

He looked over at the two beds in the room.

"Maybe." He let go of her, walked away, and sat on the edge of the one bed. "I wish this room had one bed. I really loved holding you in my arms."

"Is this the part where I'm supposed to swoon?"

He laughed. "Maybe that's what I really like about you. There's an inner strength about you. There are plenty of females who would love to get me in bed for a little fun."

"And… And I wouldn't?" She sat beside him.

"Yeah, it's fun. I won't deny that. But I'm looking for someone who is more than just a… I want something that will last…someone who understands what I do and wants to do it with me. Someone who knows how to be a woman and knows something about honor."

She put her fingers to his lips. "Don't ask me to be too honorable. You're one sexy male and a cocky one, too."

"Does that mean you want to do more than sleep?"

"Sleep? I'd love to roll in the hay with you, but I won't because I've got to look at myself in the mirror the next morning." She touched his cheek.

"That's not why I asked you to come with me. I figured it would be a really good way for you to get to know me and for you to see where I'm going when I graduate." He propped a booted foot over his knee and grabbed at the ankle. "I figured I was man enough to safely get you to the ranch without a bunch of hormones kicking in."

"So are you trying to tell me that you want me in your bed?"

He looked up and grinned. "Yeah, for as long as we live, but let's get to Wyoming first, because I don't want to screw up my chances with you."

She looked at the bed they were sitting on. "I like being in your arms. But I'm trying to...oh, how do I say this without sounding like a...I'm waiting for that special guy."

"Saving it for marriage?"

"Ideally, yeah."

"Not what I wanted to hear, but I'll give you my word and respect your commitment."

*

After spending two nights in that horrible little motel room, Jeremy pushed his way to the ranch. They arrived after midnight and tiptoed to his room. They had almost made it when his mom opened her bedroom door.

"Jeremy, you made it! I've been so worried about

you."

"We've been on the road since four a.m., I'll tell you in the morning."

"But Hannah..."

"We're too tired to care."

Jeremy stripped to his underwear and tried to watch Hannah do the same. He barely remembered Hannah curling against this chest. But when he opened his eyes, their legs were tangled, and he had his arm around her. He didn't want to rush into anything. He wanted to be absolutely certain, and he wanted her to feel the same way. For four nights, they had slept in each other's arms without doing anything more. Not that he didn't think about sex or want it, but this was about trust and respect.

He slipped out of bed and readied for the day. He joined his family at the kitchen table and took a good bit of razzing from Derrick over Hannah spending the night with him. He finally held up his hands and looked over his shoulder to be certain Hannah wasn't in earshot. "I really like Hannah. She's special, and she's what I want for a wife."

⚹

Hannah slipped into some clean but slightly wrinkled clothes and made her way downstairs. A beautiful tall pine stood in the living room and twinkled with hundreds of tiny lights, and dozens of fancy packages were tucked under it. She never considered her parents to be poor, but she'd never seen such wealth. There was nothing conceited or pretentious about Jeremy, yet she'd known plenty of kids who were total snobs.

She looked out the large windows over white fields that seemed to go on forever. The ranch had to be huge as he had told her last night when they had entered the Lazy A + 8 Ranch and they still drove forever to reach the house. Once inside the house, they had made their way through the house to his room by strategically placed nightlights that glowed across the floors and illuminated every step on the staircase. She had no clue how big or beautiful the place was, until she saw his bedroom in the morning light.

Sounds of laughter and the aroma of sausage drifted into the living room. She followed the sound and stopped short when she heard Jeremy's voice.

"She's special, and she's what I want for a wife. I've known her since my first day of classes at Cornell. She's not the least bit shy, but I've never even heard of her dating. I tried to ask her out a few times, but she always turned me down – always said she had to study for a test or something. When she told me she wasn't going home, I knew I had to bring her here. And what better way to get to know someone than to spend a few days driving with them."

Hannah could feel her body heating. She moved closer to the wall and listened carefully, but the voices were faint.

"We did a lot of talking. I know I'm in love with her. I don't want to blow it. She needs to come to the same conclusion. And for the record, the only thing we've done is sleep."

Hannah heard another man ask, "And how long do you think you can keep that up?"

"I'll do whatever it takes for her to see me as more than just another guy who wants to jump her."

An older voice said, "You better make some plans to sweep that filly off her feet or you'll lose her. I almost lost your grandmother because she had no clue I was madly in love with her."

"I think she knows."

"Don't think. Do it."

Hannah shook her hands at her side in an attempt to shed some tension from her body and plastered a smile on her face. *Time to meet the family.* She took a few more steps and entered the large kitchen with a handful of people sitting at a long table. "Hi, I'm Hannah."

Several men sprang to their feet, including Jeremy, who immediately offered the chair next to him. "Have a seat and I'll get you some coffee."

One by one the family introduced themselves.

She soon discovered that most of the family had already eaten and that Jeremy was waiting for her so that they could eat together. But it wasn't until after she'd had the most delicious breakfast that she'd probably ever eaten in her life, that Jeremy suggested she needed the grand tour of the ranch and to do a little riding.

She'd only ridden English a few times, so riding western was a new experience. They rode until the house vanished and all she could see in every direction were snow covered fields and distant mountains. It was unbelievably quiet, and the crispy cold air lacked the scent of pollution. Jeremy dismounted and then helped her down.

He took what looked like a horse blanket and dropped it on a piece of wooden fencing. "Have a seat. I wanted to talk to you without a dozen sets of ears listening."

She sat on the fence and looked around. "It's beautiful out here, and your grandparents' house is gorgeous. I've never seen such a tall Christmas tree in someone's home."

He nodded as he sat beside her. "I'm not trying to impress you with what my family has. We do have one of the largest ranches around here and we've always been successful. But I did want you to see the area. This is where I'm coming when I graduate. Our local vet has been counting down the days until I can take over. I think he wanted to retire the day I announced I'd been accepted to Cornell."

"Not too many students have that kind of a job waiting for them."

He tugged at the brim of his big western hat. "I'd like to have a partner. There's plenty of work."

"I'm sure there are quite a few people who would leap at the chance."

"Yeah, but I've had one person in mind for a long time. I just figured she'd think I was crazy and turn me down." He fidgeted with the brim of his hat again.

"Someone would be crazy to turn this down."

"I was kind of hoping that. But the person I wanted, well, it wasn't until a few days ago that I thought there was any real future." He turned his palm up as though to ask for her hand as he rested his on her leg.

She slipped her hand into his. "Who did you have in mind?"

He heaved a sigh and his breath showed in the cold air. "There's this gal at school..."

Freezing cold air went into her lungs and stayed there. *Jennifer Deleon. I should have known.*

"Seems I could get her to grab a pizza once in a while with me, but she'd never actually go out with me. Always too busy studying or something. I gave up. But right now, I figure I've got another chance with her. Seems as though we're a lot alike... We share the same values."

She watched him look away and a little part of her crumbled. Everything she had overheard at breakfast disintegrated into tiny pieces. *Maybe he wasn't talking about me.* Gathering up her courage, she knew she'd survive. He'd always been a friend. Not anything more than a friend, but a friend. At least she could say she'd spent Christmas with him, and being here was still better than being alone in her apartment.

He turned back to her and smiled. "You know, men get in trouble because women seem to think we grunt like cavemen and only toss out three word sentences. That's not true, but sometimes like now... Well, I don't want to fail. I don't want to mess things up." He swallowed. "I don't want to say the wrong thing."

"Why don't you grab your phone and ask her? What's to mess up? Just call her and tell her you've already got a job here when you graduate and you're looking for a partner. Tell her that you want HER to be your partner." She touched her fingertips to her eyes. "This cold really does get to my eyes."

"You get used to it."

He took his phone out of his pocket and swiped the screen a few times. "Just call her?"

Hannah nodded, let go of his hand, and slipped from where she was sitting. "I'll give you some privacy. Just ask her. Just blurt it out. Don't try to make it flowery. It's a business proposition. Act professional."

He nodded and smiled. "Professional. I can do that."

She walked to where the horses were tied to a railing and let a few tears slip down her cheeks. *I want you, Jeremy. That's why I consented to this insane trip. Not Jennifer. She wants her worm-filled organic garden and to make homemade vegan food for her furry friends. Little Miss Fashion Forward. I can't see her standing next to a pile of manure. She only cares about the bloodline of a horse.*

Her phone rang and she answered it. "Hello."

"Hi, it's Jeremy. I've got an offer for you. Would you be interested in accepting a veterinary position in the middle of nowhere in Wyoming? I need a partner. And you're beautiful, sexy, and I'm madly in love with you."

"Jeremy, you called me. I'm not Jennifer." She ended the call and slipped the phone into her coat pocket. Tears streamed down her face faster than she could wipe them away. Then she felt Jeremy's hands on her shoulders.

"I didn't call Jennifer. I called you. These last few days together confirmed everything I ever knew about you. I don't just want a professional partner. I want a life-long partner – someone who will love the ranch, and this way of life as much as I do. I want that person to be you."

She snuffled and tried to push away more tears.

Jeremy handed her a navy blue bandana.

She shook her head, fished in her pocket for a paper napkin that she was certain was stuffed there, and upon finding it, she blew her nose. "Me? You want me?"

He pushed a stray lock of hair from her face. "Yeah, you. We've got some time on our side before you commit. There's a whole lot of family you still haven't met. Why do you think we have such a big kitchen table?"

"I figured it was huge like everything else in that house."

Jeremy chuckled. "I'll call Doc Medino. Maybe we can pal around with him while we're here. It'll give you a better idea of what it's like working in a ranching community. I'm sure he'd like to meet you."

"Jeremy."

"Yeah?"

"You're crazy, and I'm so glad I said yes to coming with you. But please, I don't ever want to drive through another blizzard. Can we go back to the house now? I'm freezing."

"This is Wyoming. Are you wearing long johns or just those skimpy underpants that I saw in your suitcase."

"The skimpiest ones that I own. A thong made of green lace."

"Hannah, you're killing me!"

*

Christmas morning, Jeremy watched Hannah's face when she discovered packages under the tree for her.

His parents had bought her a pair of western boots. She slipped her feet into them and apparently they fit perfectly. The look of joy on her face was priceless.

"I love them. I don't have the words to express how you've made me feel."

Jeremy's mom answered, "To us, you're family."

But her cheeks turned bright pink when she opened the box from Jeremy. He had bought her a half dozen pairs of long johns, but the very bottom of the box contained a white lace thong with a matching skimpy bra.

He fingered a wayward lock of hair that had drifted over her shoulder and whispered in her ear, "Do I get to see them on you?"

She raised her eyebrows and glared at him.

He couldn't hold back his laughter. He reached in his pocket and slipped a tiny ring from the confines. "If you're not going to wear those for me, will you at least consider wearing this for now? We can make everything official with a real engagement ring after we've graduated."

He took her hand in his and slipped a tiny gold band with several small diamonds embedded in it onto her finger.

She looked at him and smiled.

Jeremy knew this was the best Christmas he'd ever

had. This was the start of his future and that future included Hannah. "Merry Christmas to my future partner."

"Merry Christmas to the most wonderful guy I've ever known." And then she kissed him.

He wrapped his arms around her. She was everything to him.

Fini

Christmas at Mariner's Cove

Chapter 1

*C*eline Colburn considered herself lucky because she had a good job; not just one good job, but two good jobs. Four days a week, she worked at home from her computer, billing patients for a national laboratory. Then on Thursday, Friday, and Saturday nights, she was a waitress at a little place called Crabby's Pot House. Her tips were usually double her day job. Between the two, she made more than probably most people her age in Mariner's Cove.

She turned off her computer, took a quick shower, and dressed in her uniform. Apparently she was supposed to look like some sort of whaling wench. To her, it looked more like a German dirndl. It had a black skirt, white blouse that was cut low, and a red vest that laced in the front. The skirt was shorter than she preferred to wear, and the blouse showed more cleavage than she liked. But she had worked the job long enough to know how to take care of herself, treat the customers well, and get good tips. And it was those tips that made life easy for her. Tips bought her car, paid for vacations, manicures, and anything else she wanted.

For the time being, she was counting down the days until March 1, when she intended to take a nice long vacation. Living in a little lobster town meant tourists came from the end of May until Christmas. From January to May, the town was so quiet it almost wasn't worth her working. But she had worked for Crabby since she was sixteen. There wasn't a job in the little restaurant that she didn't know how to do. But waiting tables was fun, as she got a kick out of flirting with the patrons.

It was October, and the town was decorated with pumpkins, gourds, and pretty autumn flowers. Those same colors were echoed in the autumn leaves that clung to the trees. She thought about the tourists who were looking for some sort of New England experience, as though they could be transported back in time when things were simpler. *Right, as though they'd give up their smart phones.*

She laughed to herself as she pulled on her heavy parka and closed the door of her apartment behind her. The short walk to the restaurant never really bothered her, except on afternoons like this one. Unseasonably cold air whipped around her. The dampness went straight to her bones. She pulled her scarf over her nose as she walked to the cove. Three blocks towards the cove and two blocks down put her at Crabby's Pot House. But on days like this, it felt like three miles. She looked over the harbor, the boats rocked at their moorings as though they wanted to free themselves of the ropes that held them. Waves smashed against the stone bulkhead, sending salty spray into the air. Bits of ocean foam blew onto the roadway that surrounded the cove. She hadn't checked the weather report, but it looked like a nor'easter. That wasn't good for the town, or for the men who made their living off the ocean.

Shop windows were bedecked in fall colors, and Mason's was no different. The dress shop was known for its expensive apparel, and as she walked past the glass windows, she drooled over the pretty red sweater set. If only she had that kind of money, but even if she did, where would she wear such a thing? She stopped for a moment and stared at the sweater, imagining the soft wool against her skin. The mannequin also sported a fancy scarf printed with colorful autumn leaves. That sweater paired with a nice pair of black slacks would be perfect for a holiday gala, except no one asked her to those kinds of parties. After all, she was nothing more than a billing clerk and part-time beer wench.

Her head filled with thoughts of the small town's inhabitants. There were those with unbelievable money, mostly retired people. Then there were those folks who were the working middle class. The watermen and their families were a tight knit group. Many of the town's residents had roots that went back to when the town was a major whaling port. She was a loner. She didn't fit with any of them.

A blast of cold air coming off the water made her turn her face towards another shop, except this was the accounting office of Brook Brooklyn. The window was decorated in nautical antiques surrounding an old lobster pot, and clusters of potted chrysanthemums, various sized pumpkins and gourds filled in all the empty spaces. The Brooklyn family could have probably afforded to buy the entire town, but Brook lived quietly in an apartment over his office. She pondered the man's name. It was odd to think of a man by the name of Brook, but it suited him.

Upon reaching the small restaurant, she pulled

open the heavy doors and stepped inside the little vestibule. A sign stood in the center of the tiny room that said SORRY WE ARE CLOSED UNTIL 5:00 PM. Yanking open another heavy door allowed her to step inside the darkened restaurant. Giving herself a moment for her eyes to adjust, she then made her way to the swinging doors of the kitchen. In an alcove behind the kitchen was a bank of lockers. Hers was the third one on the right. She unlocked the skinny metal door, as she shrugged off her coat and placed everything inside her cubical.

"Glad to see you, CeCe." The chef had nicknamed her that because all paperwork and orders contained employees' initials, and the way she made her C with a little hook on the end... Well, the name stuck. Now most everyone around Mariner's Cove called her CeCe. "Don't go getting any idears about quitting this job."

"Why? What's up?" she answered the chef. His Bostonian accent drove her crazy. Words that should have had an r sound were missing them, yet it seemed he randomly added the sound to other words.

"Well, Candy quit on Monday, and that t'igge'ed Emily and Amander to also quit."

"Who is working?" A feeling of panic rushed through her still partially frozen body.

The chef laughed. "You, Andy, and Liser."

"I hope you're joking."

"Soh'ry, wish I was."

She stood staring at the chef's back as his words sank into her. With only her and Lisa on the floor, and Andy bartending, Celine knew she was facing a grueling night. She blew a long breath out between pursed lips. *Of all weekends for Crabby to take off.* Then hollered, "Is Lisa here yet?"

"Yeah," the young dishwasher answered. "She went out to talk to Andy."

"Andy is going to have to help."

The chef laughed. "Good luck with that. You know he hates coming out f'om behind the bah'."

She tied the small black apron around her waist, gathered up her order pad, stuffed it in an apron pocket, and walked out of the kitchen.

Tiny spotlights recessed in the bar's ceiling shown on overhead glassware. Andy and Lisa were busy polishing glasses and hanging them in the proper slots over the bar. Celine sucked in a deep breath and forced a smile as she approached the bar. "Got another cloth?"

Andy tossed her a clean microfiber towel. "We certainly can use all the help we get tonight. You think you can do it?"

Celine looked at Lisa. "Are you up to it?"

Lisa shrugged. "Considering I've never actually waitressed, I have no clue."

Celine pressed her lips together for a moment. "I hate to ask, but are you old enough to serve alcohol?"

"Yes. I turned twenty-one in September."

"Thank goodness. Okay, I've worked here since I was sixteen. I started out in the back washing dishes, worked my way to hostess, and eventually I started serving. I've never seen us this shorthanded. It's going to take everything we have to keep this place running smoothly tonight, but I think we can do it. Smile, apologize if necessary, tell them up front we are shorthanded, and just remember, keep your cool, because if you do, you'll make some money in tips tonight. People will feel sorry for you as long as you give them good service. This town is bulging in leaf lookers. They are coming down east expecting a great seafood meal, great service, and we need to deliver it to them." She turned to Andy. "You're going to have to help. I know you don't want to do anything other than tend bar, but you're going to have to help serve."

"Sorry, CeCe, no can do. I'm a bartender." Andy 's pirate uniform looked as though it had been custom designed for him. His dark hair was pulled into a ponytail, long sideburns, and five o'clock shadow made him look very handsome.

When Andy wasn't working as a bartender, he served as the town's police detective. The old-fashioned pistol on his hip was real, just not a police issue, and Celine never asked if it was loaded or not. She assumed it was.

Celine thought it was funny to watch the women who would flirt with him. Andy would play along and flirt back, but Andy was more of a girl than they were.

"Tonight you will be more than just a bartender. You will serve and you will help out. Lisa can't do it all by herself."

"That's your job."

Celine shot Andy her meanest look. "You can at least serve those in the bar."

"I can't be running to the back."

"We'll get it to you and you can serve it." Celine walked over and turned up the lights in the dining room. The room glowed in soft lighting that was meant to mimic candlelight.

At eleven thirty that evening, Andy put out the last call for drinks. Somehow they had all survived. None of the patrons complained and everything appeared to have gone smoothly. Celine cleaned up her tables, wiped everything down, and ran an electric broom over the floor. She couldn't remember ever being that busy. But one patron stood out in her mind. She fished in her apron pocket and found the business card he had left with his outrageous tip. Franklin Cresson of Brooklyn, Brooklyn, Cresson, and Fields law offices. He had left her his name, a phone number, and the hefty tip.

Franklin was tall, with golden blond hair, and even in the low lighting of the restaurant, Celine could tell that Franklin had the prettiest blue eyes. Any other night, she would've flirted with him, but tonight she barely had time to be polite. *Omigosh, he was handsome.*

She had been honest with him about being short staffed from the moment she seated him.

He smiled and told her he understood.

She wasn't certain of his age and figured he was at least in his late twenties. Maybe if she carded him, she would've known exactly his age, but the only thing he ordered was coffee. Now she wished he'd ordered a beer. The alcohol beverage law suggested that anyone who looked under forty should be carded. There was something about him. He looked familiar, as if she'd known him.

As soon as she was certain the restaurant's dining room was clean and tidy, she went to the kitchen. The chef had left and the dishwasher was cleaning up. She closed out the main register, double checked the money, recorded it on a deposit slip, bundled the cash, register tally, and bank slip in a zip bag and placed it into the safe. Andy still had his register to count, but that was not her problem. She emptied her pockets in her apron and stashed her tip money in her coat pocket. Alone in her apartment, she would count what she made tonight. There was no question in her mind that she had done well.

If the walk to the little restaurant was cold, the walk home was twice as cold. Her apartment was on the second floor of an old house that her parents owned. It was where she'd grown up. Before her parents moved to Louisiana, they spilt the house into two living quarters. Celine stayed in the upstairs, and a young family rented the downstairs.

Most of the year-round residents had lived in Mariner's Cove all their lives. She was relatively a newcomer. Her parents were actually from Florida, but moved to Mariner's Cove shortly after she was born. Her father's job as a buyer for a major frozen food company was always subject to change, and change it did. When he got his promotion, she was in high school and didn't want to leave.

Her mom stayed in Mariner's Cove while her dad spent three years in Maryland. He drove home to

Mariner's Cove on weekends and holidays. But when he was transferred to Louisiana, Celine stayed behind. Her parents were leery about leaving her. Thrilled to be on her own, she'd grown up in Mariner's Cove, knew everyone, and was comfortable here.

Quietly she climbed the stairs to her apartment, pulled off her coat and hung it in her hall closet. She'd call Rachel in the morning and see if there were any way the young woman would consider coming back. She had quit last June when she had married. Celine knew they were too shorthanded to face a Friday or Saturday night, during a peak tourist season.

She counted her tip money twice. Never had she made that much in a single night. She put her money in a zip bag and stuffed it in the freezer compartment of her refrigerator behind the ice cube bucket. Tomorrow she'd deposit it in the bank. She laughed to herself. *Maybe I'll buy that pretty red sweater after all.*

She picked up the business card Frank Cresson had left and fingered it for a second before dropping it on her kitchen table. *Does he want me to call him?*

The next morning, Celine was phoning everyone she knew, trying to find another waitress. Finally a guy by the name of Lloyd said he'd be willing to fill in for a few nights.

"Great! Wear black slacks and a white shirt."

"Dress shirt? I don't own one."

"Got a plain white tee shirt?"

"Yeah."

"Wear it. I'll meet you at four sharp." Celine knew they were still short, but not as short as they were last night, and Friday night was always a big night for restaurants.

At four, Lloyd walked through the back door. He had no experience as a waiter, but he had plenty of customer service experience working at the grocery store.

"Here." She handed him a red scarf to tie around his neck and gave him an apron. He caught on quickly to where everything was, and deep inside, Celine knew he'd do well. She had him fill out the necessary paperwork, and although she had no authority to do so, she hired him.

By five thirty, they were backed up with a wait time of at least forty-five minutes. She didn't care. At least, there was enough wait staff to keep the restaurant going. But when Franklin Cresson came in for a table, she seated him at a small high-top table in the bar. The place was overflowing in tourists.

Mentally she crossed her fingers and hoped that tonight's tips would be as good as the previous night. People liked choosing a lobster from the big tank. She'd reach in with large tongs and capture it. After it was tagged, she would send it to the back where it was weighed, steamed, and served. She felt sorry for the little creatures. In fact, anything with eyeballs made her think twice before eating it. It was one thing to see a steak on a plate, and another to see the steer.

The night was insanely busy, and trying to find a moment to flirt with Franklin was next to impossible. Often the most she was capable of doing was giving him a little wink as she passed by, while getting drinks for another table. But Franklin smiled, and his smile warmed her.

The place was still hopping at ten o'clock, but she stopped for a moment by Franklin to say hello. "Hi, glad to see you're back. How was dinner?"

"Great. Except I was hoping to have you as a waitress."

"Thanks. But if you had waited for me, you'd probably still be waiting. I assumed you were hungry."

"I was. Will you call me?"

"I work a lot of hours, and I have a feeling I'll be

working all next week. That puts a damper on my social life."

Franklin chuckled. "I understand. I'm going to be here for a while. I took a few weeks off. Give me a call, and we'll find some time."

"Are you related to Brook Brooklyn?"

"Yes. I'm his younger cousin."

She smiled, held up her hand, and wiggled her fingers. "Gotta get back to work."

She wondered why someone like him would take an interest in her. But it was fun to think that she had captured the attention of someone similar to Brook. She glanced at Franklin one more time before entering the kitchen. She had no idea why someone with his money would even be remotely attracted to her, and she had no desire to be a rich boy's toy. She giggled to herself as she collected another round of plates from the chef. *But, I wonder what it would be like to be spoiled by a wealthy guy.*

⁂

Frank watched the young woman walk away. He couldn't explain what it was about her that held him captive. But she had.

He hadn't been in Mariner's Cove in years, not since that summer after he'd hurt his leg during a motocross competition. The injury had bought him an extra semester of college. It was a hard lesson. He tried not to think about that summer and the strain it had placed on his relationship with Brook. But in the years that followed, Frank realized he'd grown up and changed. And now he somewhat understood why Brook had left the law firm. In the beginning, Frank got a kick out of winning cases, but soon the fun was gone. The courtroom couldn't compare to the thrill of motocross, and to some extent, he was an adrenalin junkie. He was ready for a change of pace, and Mariner's Cove had called to him.

Yet in the back of his mind, he began to wonder if Mariner's Cove was actually another mistake. He had arrived on Brook' s doorstep and begged to be allowed to use the yacht. Brook appeared to be cordial enough, but Frank could tell that the relationship between them was still strained. Even Nikki, Brook's wife, failed to welcome him - he'd been a jerk that summer, and he knew it.

Brook was always the older, wiser, and the most reliable of all the cousins in the family. Frank almost destroyed Brook's chance at happiness by hinting to Nikki that Brook was gay. Plus there was that fiasco with Brook's daughter. There were several times that Frank tried to tell his cousin that he was sorry, but Brook wasn't interested in an apology. Looking back, Frank knew he had given his cousin every reason to be angry. He was hoping it would all be water under the bridge. Except it wasn't.

He tossed some money on the table and left the small restaurant. The walk to the yacht in the rain did nothing to help his already soured mood. Once on the ship, he grabbed a Coors Lite and headed for the bedroom. The ship rocked and moaned against the ties that held her in place. *This town doesn't need a major storm.*

When the last patron left the small restaurant, Celine locked up and wiped the tables. Every swipe with the germicidal laden cloth seemed to pull at her aching shoulder muscles. She only wanted to finish and tumble into her bed. Looking around the room, she decided that the place was as clean as it would get. There was no energy left in her. She grabbed her coat from her locker and stepped out into the cold, wet night.

Lights surrounded the small harbor illuminating both pleasure and workboats, but through the driving rain, they were barely visible. The din of a million raindrops slapping the cobblestone walkway that surrounded the harbor and paved street, drown the sounds of the boats in their moorings. A wave splashed against the bulkhead and tossed water into the street. Celine shuddered and scurried towards her apartment.

She practically threw her body against her door as her apartment key protruded from her fingertips. It took a second to insert the key into the lock. The sound of rain hid the familiar click of the tumbler releasing. She pushed the door open and quickly closed it. She shrugged out of her rain-drenched clothing and scampered to find her robe. A few seconds later, she stood in the warm shower, washing away the scent of seafood and sloshed beer.

Her nightly routine was down pat. She stepped out of the shower, dried her hair, brushed her teeth, flossed, and put on her flannel nightgown. After straightening the bathroom, she cleaned up the wet clothing she had left in the foyer, and wiped the wooden floor dry. Then she sat and counted her tips. *Whoa, it's been one heck of a night.* To be certain, she counted her money again. Bundled in a zip bag, she put her tips in the freezer. She thought Thursday night had been good, but Friday night had been twice as good. Her mind wandered to Franklin, and she smiled.

She definitely liked the attention. Tall and handsome, there hadn't been one woman in the bar who hadn't noticed him. But he seemed to be watching her. Then she chided herself. She wasn't the kind of woman that men chased. Mariner's Cove was crawling with good-looking young women from wealthy families. Women, who had careers in Boston and New York, but enjoyed spending time away from it all. They liked hanging out at the antique shops, visiting the seafaring museum, combing the art galleries, and drinking wine with their friends on the patios of the fancy cafés that faced the harbor. She wasn't one of them, just a small town, hard-working gal. But something about Franklin warmed her. And being the analytical person that she was, she came right back to the question: why me?

*

Sun shone brightly and Frank winced against the bright light coming through the porthole. He wasn't certain how he managed to find sleep. The yacht had spent most of the night protesting the ropes holding it tight to the dock. He threw back the covers and slipped into an old pair of jeans before making his way topside. Sunlight glistened on the water like a gazillion diamonds. Most of the fishing and lobster boats had already left. Squinting against the light, he went to the not so tiny galley and made a pot of coffee. In spite of the sun, the cool air accosted him. He shivered. While the coffee brewed, he returned to the bedroom and looked through his clothing, until he found his cotton cable sweater, and pulled it over his head. He loved New England in the fall. And being on the yacht, held special appeal. He poured a cup of coffee, and went topside to watch the town wake up from its slumber.

He started to formulate plans for the day. The rain had washed the small town and now it seemed to glow in shades of red and orange. Even the cobblestones that surrounded the cove seemed bright and clean. The sun beat down on his shoulders, yet the air was nippy and scented with salt and fish. He couldn't remember a morning he had enjoyed more.

Looking across the way, he spotted CeCe's long chestnut ponytail. It would be difficult to mistake her in a crowd. Although average in looks, when put together, she was extremely attractive. The mane that hung down her back seemed to almost emulate the fall colors around her. Her tight fitting jeans accented the healthy curves of her well-muscled legs and derrière. The sloppy fitting sweatshirt in bright yellow, printed with an iridescent orange lobster down her back, looked like something that belonged in the trash. Yet on her, it added to her carefree, sexy appearance.

Frank raised his hands above his head and let out a sharp whistle. "CeCe!"

She didn't even look in his direction. He stood, raised his voice, and tried again. Still to no avail, he slipped his feet into his dock shoes and took off down the pier towards the town's buildings. He caught up with her by the bank. Slightly out of breath, he managed to choke out, "Hi."

CeCe beamed him a big smile. "Hi, yourself. You're up early."

"So are you. It's a beautiful morning."

"It is. After yesterday, this is exactly the kind of weather the tourists love."

Fully recovered from his run, he shot her his best smile. "This is the kind of weather I love."

They stood there looking at each other. Frank never felt such a loss for words. She was sans all makeup. Big brown eyes were surrounded with long eyelashes, and her cheeks glowed a peachy pink in the crispy air. He mentally crossed his fingers and tried not to stammer. "Would you care for some breakfast?"

"Oh my, what a delicious invitation, but I just ate a granola bar before I walked out of the house."

"Ah, can I at least interest you in a cup of coffee?"

"I think I would enjoy that." She looked up at him.

He felt incredibly tall next to her. He hadn't realized how short she was. "Well, follow me. I probably have the best coffee in town."

They walked back to the yacht and he helped her on board. He wanted to laugh as her eyes scanned the interior. The multimillion-dollar yacht was the epitome of luxury. He poured her a cup of coffee and then offered to give her the grand tour. When they reached the main bedroom, he groaned, "I'm sorry, I wasn't expecting company."

"That's all right. I haven't made my bed either. I was trying to do a few things before the streets became too crowded with tourists. The buses start bringing them in around nine."

"I noticed." He led her back to where he had been sitting when he first saw her. "I don't think I'm going to stay on the yacht all winter, but I haven't decided what I'm going to do."

"If I could live on the yacht like this, I'd never leave."

He laughed. "Yes you would, for the same reasons I'll leave."

"And what would that be?"

He relaxed into a deck chair and crossed his feet. "Lack of privacy, and it can get very cold on the water."

"But it's heated, right?"

"Yes, it's heated. But it's not the same as living in a house. I've been looking at a house for sale about two miles from the cove. It's a beauty - all cedar shake and quite old. It needs some work. I'm negotiating with the owners. It's outrageously priced."

"Is it on the water?" She took a sip of her coffee.

"Yes. Would you like to see it? I can call the real estate agent. I wouldn't mind looking at it again."

"I would love to, but I have to be back in time to go to work."

"Not a problem. Let me grab my phone." He returned to his bedroom, found his phone, and called the real estate office. He listened to the phone ring several times before it went into a message system. "This is Frank. I'm calling for Amanda Ilsip. I'd like to see the house again if possible around noon. Please call me back." He went to where CeCe was sitting. "Make yourself at home and have another cup coffee. I called the real estate agent. With luck, she'll call me back in a few minutes. In the meantime, let me get ready. I hate to say this, but I had just tumbled from bed when I spotted you."

CeCe drained the last of the coffee in her cup and stood. "I'm glad you did. As far as I'm concerned, being invited to drink morning coffee on your yacht is the most fantastic invitation I've ever had."

"Then let me spoil you by asking you to share a cup with me every morning."

She raised her eyebrows and cocked her head. "I'm afraid that invitation could be taken more than one way."

Frank laughed as he called over his shoulder, "That's not what I was thinking when I said it, but if that's what it takes, I would enjoy having you."

"In your dreams!"

✳

Celine listened to him laugh as he vanished into the bowels of the yacht. Somehow she didn't think that's what he meant when he'd said it. He didn't come off as a player. Something about him screamed decent guy. She fixed another cup of coffee and looked around the kitchen. *So, this is how the rich and famous live.*

A few minutes later, Franklin returned holding his phone to his ear. She listened to the one-sided conversation and could tell he was setting up an appointment to see the house. His blond hair was still slightly damp. He wore dark green khaki pants with a lighter green, long-sleeved, polo shirt that didn't hide his broad shoulders and muscular chest. He looked downright sexy.

When he said goodbye, she asked, "What's up?"

"We're to meet the agent at eleven thirty."

"Sounds like fun."

"It will be. Let's go grab an early lunch."

They walked along the cove to the old hotel. Since the lunch menu was not yet available, they settled for the breakfast. Celine looked over the various items and thought maybe she had died and gone to heaven. Never had she seen such an array of breakfast foods. From oysters Rockefeller to lobster Newburg, the menu contained so many gourmet items.

Franklin told her to get whatever she wanted.

She chose the lobstermen breakfast, which consisted of hard-boiled eggs mixed with lobster in a

Newburg sauce, which was topped with bacon. It was actually more than she could comfortably eat, but it was so creamy and delicious, she forced herself to eat every bite, leaving only a small piece of toast behind. The entire time, they chatted and laughed. Never before had she felt so genuinely at ease with someone. She didn't feel as though she was on a date, she felt as though she was with her best friend, and they had known each other for a million years.

When they were done, they walked back to the yacht. Franklin brought her a helmet.

"Ready to take a ride?"

"I've never been on a motorcycle."

"It's about time."

He talked to her about how to move with the cycle and assured her that he was a very capable driver and knew exactly what he was doing. Butterflies flitted through her stomach as she climbed on the bike and wrapped her arms around his waist. He drove through town and then onto the road that would take them to the house he was considering purchasing. It was fun and exciting, unlike anything she had ever experienced.

The house was exactly as he described, cedar shake weathered to a silver gray. The back porch slipped to a deck that seemed to go on forever, and then an expanse of grass that led to wooden stairs that put them on a wide beach. The tide was out, making the beach seem twice as large. It was a quiet spot, just them and the Atlantic Ocean. She stuck her hands in her back pockets and sniffed the air. Such incredible beauty, and it would be Franklin's - his private little place in the middle of nowhere.

He came up behind her and slipped his arms around her waist. She felt his hands, but was lost in her own delightful thoughts, until she felt his lips on the side of her neck. "I think you're moving a little too quickly. I barely know you, and I'm not that kind of woman."

"And just what kind of woman are you?"

"Let's just say I'm not going to be swept off my feet by a guy with money."

"Does that mean you're looking for a poor one?"

She giggled. "No thanks. It's all I can do to pay my own bills. I certainly don't want to be supporting someone else."

"Then let me state up front that I'm not poor. Nor am I looking for someone to support me. But I do get the feeling that there's some sort of chemistry going on between us. Like a moth being drawn to the light, I'm feeling something... Something special between us as though I've known you forever. I've felt it since I first laid eyes on you. Except I can't explain it."

She turned and stared at him. "I'm feeling it, too. But I think we need to give ourselves time. I don't want to jump into anything. Maybe I'm overly cautious?"

"I'm used to going after what I want, and I have a tendency to get exactly what I want."

"Well, this time you're going to have to go very slowly."

He ran his index finger down her cheek, across her jaw, and under her chin.

She wanted to melt on the spot because his touch was doing delicious things to her. Instead, she sucked in a deep breath and watched his eyes. "I can see that you are going to have a very difficult time doing anything slowly."

He tilted her chin upwards. His lips found hers. Her knees didn't want to hold her as the heat from his kiss warmed her entire body. He backed away from his kiss and grinned. "Slow has never been part of my vocabulary. But since you know almost nothing about me, I'll give you whatever time you need. I'll also warn you, I'm playing for keeps. My days of looking for a good time are over. I put an end to them a long time ago. I want one woman and a lifetime commitment."

Celine swallowed. Had he just said everything that she ever wanted to hear from a man?

He took her hand and they walked back to the house. The gardens were overgrown and filled with weeds, but it was obvious that at one time they had been beautiful. She couldn't wait to see the interior.

She knew the house, knew who owned it, and had heard the rumors of its asking price. The Sea View was no ordinary home. Senator Jack Chase was one of those colorful people who liked to hide in Mariner's Cove. When the news media began to flaunt stories of his bisexual kink, it forced his resignation, and permanently he had retired to Mariner's Cove. Fortunately for the little town, Jack Chase was far away when he was found dead in a hotel room. Being Jack Chase had never married and was without children, a distant family member was selling the house.

"Franklin, you do know who owned this place, don't you?" she asked as they sat on the front step.

He chuckled. "Oh, I know. I know more about the man than I want to know, after being in this house. Why do you call me Franklin?"

"Because that's what's on the card you gave me."

He threaded his fingers through hers. "Call me Frank."

"Most of the town calls me CeCe. My name is Celine Colburn."

"So which do you prefer Celine or CeCe?"

She sucked her bottom lip in and then raked her top teeth over it. "Celine... Maybe when it's just us, and in public, I'm CeCe."

He gave her hand a little squeeze.

Moments later, an SUV drove up the driveway and parked in front of the house. Amanda Ilsip stepped out and greeted them. It took her a second to unlock the door, and they all stepped into the interior of the house.

Celine sucked in a breath that she hoped wasn't audible. It was like walking into a house of some movie star. In fact, the place looked as though someone would return any moment. She wandered unhindered from room to room. Each room was meticulously decorated in an ultra modern style that was more sterile than pretty. The kitchen was large, and with all its stainless steel, the area looked more like a hospital's operating room.

She followed Frank upstairs, and when she looked into the first bedroom, she gasped. "Is that what I think it is?"

Frank chuckled. "I don't know what you're thinking, but probably. It's obvious his kink included handcuffs. Why don't you forget you ever saw it? As I said before, I now know more than I ever wanted to know about the man."

"That's one image that isn't going to leave my mind easily."

Frank took her hand in his and brought her fingers to his lips. "As far as I'm concerned, the house is going to have to be gutted. Start over fresh. Remember, it's a house. It's not responsible for what was done to it or how it was used. I want everything about Jack Chase removed."

"Good. Because the house gives me the creeps."

Frank raised his eyebrows. "Really? Does that mean that you can see yourself living here with me?"

"Oh. Um, I... Ah, oh dear. I meant... Why would anyone want..? May we leave now?"

Celine wandered outside while Frank and the real estate agent discussed the house. Celine checked her watch and knew she had plenty of time, but she wanted to rid everything she had seen in the house from her mind. When Frank joined her, she breathed a sigh of relief.

"I know I have to get you back so you can go to work."

She pulled the helmet onto her head and Frank checked the adjustment before he got on his motorcycle. She climbed on the cycle behind him and held him tight as they drove away from the house and back to the town. Giving him directions, he took her to her apartment.

She thought about inviting him up, but with an hour to get ready for work, she decided against it. He promised to see her at Crabby's. She waved goodbye as he drove off. Part of her was wrapped in the most delicious feeling of pure joy. It was as though she had found a love that had been hidden from her. Was it possible to find a real prince charming, or was her mind and body playing tricks on her?

Chapter 2

*T*he following morning, Celine stopped by the yacht. Frank was waiting for her, and so was her coffee.

"Do you work this evening?" Frank asked.

"Sunday is my one day off. I live for Sundays."

"Great. Drink your coffee and allow me to steal you for the day. Shall we play tourist and see if there's any color left in the mountains?"

"On your motorcycle?"

"I didn't bring a car up here with me."

"If that's the case, then I'd like to go home and change into something warmer."

"Not a problem." Frank looked at his phone. "If I pick you up at your place around ten, would that give you enough time?"

"Did you have anyplace specific in mind?"

"Not really. Do you know of someplace we should go?"

"There's an apple orchard about two hours northwest of here. And a charming little restaurant with home-cooked food that's off the tourist path."

"Sounds perfect!"

She looked beyond the stern of the boat towards the Atlantic. "This is home, yet getting away for the day is a real treat. See you at ten?"

*

"Not before I get a kiss." He pulled Celine to him, wrapped his arms around her, and kissed her with more than a little gusto. There was something about her that made his heart pound. When he let go of her, she scampered away. He watched her cross the street and head for her place. Being near her lifted his spirits.

Showered, shaved, and dressed in his heavy jeans and motorcycle boots, he pulled on his jacket and checked the time. With plenty to spare, he checked his cycle carefully before starting it. He loved this machine. It was top of the line. The suspension hugged the road, yet created a ride that was as smooth as the water in the cove on a calm day. He revved the engine and listened to it purr.

Ken Taylor was an old motocross buddy, and when he graduated from Rensselaer Polytech, he had one thing on his mind, his own motorcycle company. Except, he needed funding. Ken came to Frank. Knowing it was a good investment; Frank managed to finance Ken's fledging business. Frank understood motorcycles. They had been his life - his reason for living, and he also understood law. As a silent partner, he helped his buddy set up the company and watched as Ken took his concept from his dad's backyard garage to a small modern facility outside of Augusta, Maine. The partnership of Taylor and Cresson became Tayson. Ken's machines, known as Tayson Motorcycles, were taking the racing world and the riding enthusiast by storm.

Frank smiled. He was sitting on the third bike to roll off the assembly line. It was worth a fortune.

He turned on his helmet camera, checked his phone to be certain it was picking up the signal, adjusted his helmet, and dropped the shield over his face. This was one day he never wanted to forget. Just him and the most wonderful female for a Sunday drive through New England's colorful countryside.

Celine. Just thinking about her name sent a tingle through his system. "Celine Cresson, my love, my wife!"

He backed his bike from where it was parked and drove out of the parking lot. As he pulled to the signal light, Bobby Finch pulled beside him in his big pickup with a boat trailer attached to the hitch. Frank raised his hand in a friendly gesture and Bobby waved back. When the light turned green, Bobby pulled into the intersection as Frank made the right turn.

Frank spotted Celine, and her big smile, at the next intersection, but behind him was the sound of metal.

✳

It happened so fast. Celine screamed.

Having watched Frank being ejected from his bike and watching his body fly through the air before crashing into the glass panes of Shelby's antique store, sent a chill through her that held her paralyzed for a split second before sending her into motion and running towards Frank, almost unaware of the chaos that had not ended. Glass was everywhere as she stepped through the window to reach Frank.

Sirens sounded in the distance and Mrs. Shelby grabbed Celine's arm. "Don't touch him, darling. The paramedics will be here in just a moment."

"Frank!" She choked on sobs. "Frank. Oh please, Frank, don't die." She wanted to hold him in her arms and kiss him, not stand in a puddle of broken glass in Shelby's antique shop. But with the tight grip Mrs. Shelby had on Celine's arm, she knew she couldn't do a thing.

Ice was circulating in her body and she fought the foggy sensation that threatened to suck her into a gray whirlpool. Seconds seemed like forever. "Why aren't they here? He's going to die."

"No, CeCe, stop that. He's been knocked unconscious. I'm sure the blood you are seeing is from coming from all that glass. He was wearing a helmet. He'll be fine. Calm down. He's not going to die." Mrs. Shelby patted Celine on the back. "You know him?"

"Yes. It's Frank Cresson."

"Someone you met at Crabby's?"

Celine shook her head. "Not exactly. It's not what you are thinking. His cousin lives here and he's staying on his family's boat. He's buying a house here in Mariner's Cove."

"Who's his..."

The paramedics arrived and a police officer came to Celine. "Please, CeCe, would you mind stepping out here. We need to talk to you."

"I don't want to leave Frank."

"You'll be more help to him out here."

She followed the officer out the shop's front door and into the sunshine. To her left was Bobby's truck with the twisted trailer lying near the passenger side of the truck. Bobby stood next to it, scratching his head as if dazed by the whole event. She didn't see the motorcycle, only the upside down car that was precariously perched on the seawall. "Oh, dear God."

She looked up at the officer she'd known her whole life, as tears flowed over her cheeks. "How many people are hurt?"

"Four. Let's start with what you saw."

Celine tried to tell what she had seen, but her focus had been on Frank and not on anything else. She looked behind her and realized the paramedics were working on Frank. "May I have his cell phone? I need the phone numbers for his family. I don't want to call his office."

One of the paramedics handed her a small bag. "You'll have to sign that you took his personal things."

She nodded. "Please, I want to go with him to

Regional Hospital."

The deafening sound of a medical transport helicopter hovering overhead caused her to cover her ears. She watched the helicopter land on an open stretch of beach on the northern shore of the cove. She raised her voice and shouted, "Why are they so far away?"

"It's too dangerous to have them attempt to land here."

She watched the paramedics lift the stretcher containing Frank and place him in the ambulance. "Please, I want to go with him."

"No, CeCe. You can't. They are air lifting him to General. Regional doesn't have the facilities to handle this sort of an accident. Let them do what they must. You can drive down to General later. Sign here," the officer said.

"What am I signing?"

"This one is for your statement," he flipped the page, "and this one is for his personal effects. You'll be responsible for every single penny."

"I'm not stealing from him!"

"CeCe, calm down. This isn't the big city. I shouldn't allow you to have it, but I trust you."

Her gaze scanned the street. "Where's his motorcycle?"

The officer pointed.

Down the block, in the exact spot where she had been standing on the sidewalk, lay the purple, royal blue, and black cycle on its side. "Will you help me put it back in his parking place by the docks?"

"CeCe, that cycle is going to our locked impound. One, it's been in an accident, and two, that's no ordinary cycle, that's a Tayson. I can't believe he parked it in the lot. Do you know what that is worth?"

She shrugged. "Twenty thousand?"

The older officer shook his head. "Half the guys on the force would pay that amount, plus give their right arm and first born just to take that baby for a spin." He shoved his thumb over his shoulder. "There are very few pleasure boats out there that cost as much as that cycle. You'd think it was made of solid gold."

"Why didn't they take his helmet off?"

"Not certain, but I think they wait for the doctors to do that in case there's a head injury."

"Is he going to be okay?"

"CeCe, again, calm down. He's alive, and they are doing everything they can for him."

She couldn't help it. She couldn't stop the quiver in her stomach. She couldn't keep her hands from shaking. From where she stood, she was unable to see the paramedics load Frank into the helicopter. She wondered if the helicopter would wait for the other victims to be extricated from the overturned vehicle. With her attention focused on the inverted car, she watched as a tow truck began to stabilize the vehicle, while another crew prepared to cut open the car. Suddenly her whole body began to shake as though it had turned freezing cold. "May I go home?"

"Certainly. If I need anything else, I'll call you."

She walked down the block and looked at the motorcycle. She knew Frank loved it. He'd be upset to think it was resting there on its side. Then she crossed under the police tape and walked home. She opened her door and ran up the staircase and into the apartment.

A stray thought drifted through her mind. She had not seen Brook or Nikki in the crowd. Had they somehow missed what had happened? She grabbed her phone and called Brook's office. The phone rang quite a few times before sending her to a voice message system that said the office was closed on Sundays.

Foiled, she grabbed for Frank's phone in the package of personal items. When she touched the screen, she realized she was watching the events happening on the street, except the picture wasn't very clear. Confusion clouded her mind as she fought to make sense of what she was seeing. Then it registered and everything fell into place. The only possible explanation was that Frank was wearing a helmet cam and had intended to record the entire day's events. Her heart swelled at the thought of what could've been before it seemingly shattered and fell into the pit of her stomach. Tears rolled down her cheeks, and for once, she had the luxury of crying unchecked. Finding her box of tissues, she wiped her face and blew her nose. Then she wet a paper towel with cool water and wiped her face. *Crying isn't helping him.*

Celine looked at Frank's phone still showing the events on the street. *I've got to find that camera.*

She ran down her staircase and the three blocks to where the accident had taken place. Police tape surrounded everything. She ducked under the tape and a police officer attempted to stop her.

"It's okay. I was in this accident. I need to talk to Officer Crawley. I'm going to wait for him over there," she pointed to the far end of the seawall, "a fair distance from the overturned car."

She crossed the street and looked for anything that might have been a camera. She spotted several small pieces of litter and a bag from a fast food restaurant, which angered her. *I don't throw trash in your yard, but you think you can throw it in mine?*

As she drew back her foot to kick the bag, she noticed a tiny black thing. She checked the phone and put her foot in front of the bag. *Bingo!*

She dropped her keys in front of the bag and then leaned over and picked them up along with the small black box. Then pocketed both.

"You wanted to talk to me?" Officer Crawley said.

Her heart flew to her throat. Guilt assaulted her, knocking the wind from her lungs. Knowingly tampering with a crime scene... She prayed she wouldn't be arrested. "Um, I thought of something that I didn't tell you."

The officer stared at her.

"We were going to go to Clifford's Orchard, and, um I, um, didn't tell you that and I didn't know if, I mean, I, um..."

"That doesn't matter. I'm certain you will hear from the Commonwealth Attorney."

She pointed her thumb over her shoulder towards the overturned car. "What about them?"

"I'm not a medic, but there's no reason at the moment to think that they won't make it. They're a little bloody, but they are laughing and having a grand time."

Part of her wanted to go over to that car and

scream at them. To them, this was fun? A bunch of spoiled teens in a hot sports car - too drunk or high to realize what they'd done, or the danger that they are in. She shook her head as she walked away.

When she was nine, she had spent the summer with her paternal grandmother. That summer stood out in her mind as being her favorite childhood memory. Her grandmother was a little spitfire and full of energy, in spite of battling cancer. That grandmother had been a young war bride. And over the next twenty years, managed to have six boys. The woman had amazing inner strength and fortitude. Celine could almost hear her grandmother saying, 'Don't grab the bull by the horns when things go awry, grab him by the nose and control the situation.' *I need to take control.*

Back in her apartment, she hooked a USB cord to the camera, downloaded a copy of the video to her computer, and then she watched it.

Frank smiled into the camera. She turned the sound up just in time to hear Frank say, "Today I'm taking Mrs. Franklin Cresson for a ride. I cannot imagine being more in love than I am with Celine. She is absolutely the perfect wife for me." A moment later, the video showed Frank leaving the parking lot as he said, "Celine Cresson, my love, my wife!"

A most wonderful tingly feeling filled her. *He loves me as much as I love him.*

Her hands were shaking so hard she wasn't certain she'd be able to fix a cup of coffee, but somehow she managed to insert the little pod into the coffeemaker. Pressing start, she grabbed her mug from the old fashion drainer that sat next to the sink and pushed it under the spout. The little machine made a familiar gurgle and hissed a few times before the dark brown liquid began to drip into the mug.

She stuck the tip of her teaspoon into the sugar bowl, sprinkled a few grains into her coffee, and then added a dash of heavy cream before stirring. Taking a few sips of her hot coffee, she began to formulate some plans. If she went to the hospital, she knew no one would allow her near Frank if she said she was his friend. A grin pulled her cheeks. *If I go as his wife... I need perfection. I need to look like I'm Frank's wife.*

When her grandmother died, her father's oldest brother's wife handled the woman's estate. At the time, Celine was just shy of her twelfth birthday. That aunt sent Celine, the only female on her father's side, a wedding ring set, a double strand of pearls, a complete set of antique china plates, and the sterling silverware that went with it.

She reached into her jewelry box and found the antique ring set that had belonged to her grandmother. The setting was ornate and old-fashioned. Celine slipped the set on her left ring finger and held up her hand. They were a hair's breadth loose, but she could wear them. She pulled them off long enough to drop them into a jar of jewelry cleaner.

Then she worked on finding the perfect outfit. Frustration began to build in her like a geyser. She searched her closet one more time, settled on a pair of chocolate-brown corduroy pants, and paired them with a yellow sweater. Then she searched her jewelry box. Not finding what she wanted, she searched her top bureau drawer that was filled with little boxes of odd jewelry. Positive that the little pin had to be in one of those boxes, she searched a second time. This time she carefully checked the box that contained several pieces of wooden jewelry, and there she found it. Underneath a chunkier piece sat the little, copper enamel leaf brooch with matching earrings.

Taking the leaf jewelry to the bathroom, she put them on, and stared at herself in the mirror. *Certainly Frank's wife would wear some makeup.* She applied a little eye shadow, mascara, and lip-gloss. *Perfect.* She reached into the jar of jewelry cleaner, gave the rings a good brushing with the tiny jar's brush, rinsed the rings, and placed them on her finger. She held her hand up and admired the antique diamond setting and how the diamonds sparkled in the bathroom light. *Thank you, Grandmother.*

She slipped her feet into a little pair of flatties, grabbed up her phone and Frank's.

I can do this. I must! She called Brook's office number and waited. This time, Nikki answered the phone.

"Oh, Nikki, I am so glad I was able to reach you. This is CeCe Colburn. I'm calling about Frank. He's been in an accident. They airlifted him to General."

"I saw there was an accident on the street, but I had no idea Frank was involved. How is he?"

"I really don't know. I'm headed to the hospital now." Celine flew down the stairs, slamming the door behind her as she made a dash for her car. "I'll call back as soon as I know something." She took a deep breath. "Will you do me a favor? Will you call Frank's mother?"

"Yes, of course. Brook isn't here. He took his daughter for a little one-on-one time."

Celine started her car. "I've got to hang up. I can't drive and talk."

"No problem. I'll try to get hold of Brook and let

him know. And I'll call Frank's mom. Thank you for calling me."

Celine put the phone beside her on the seat. She figured it would take her at least an hour to get to Eastern General Hospital. Taking a few deep breaths, she flexed her fingers over the steering wheel, and said a little prayer for Frank and for her. She might have to give the performance of a lifetime, but first, she had to get there safely.

The ride to the hospital seemed to take forever, and once there, all she could do was wait. Two hours became four and four slipped into six. Finally a doctor came to her.

"Mrs. Cresson, we've done everything we can do. It is now up to Frank to recover."

"What exactly does that mean?"

"There was quite a bit of brain trauma. We've done everything we can to relieve the pressure, but until Frank wakes up, we really won't know just how bad or if there's any damage."

"Damage...? As in vegetable?"

"Ma'am, there's no way of telling at this time. Let's not even think about that. He's a healthy young male and that much is in his favor. What happens from now onwards is between him and God."

The doctor stared hard into Celine's eyes. "Stay

focused on a complete recovery. Don't let him think that he's not coming through this perfectly fine. This is going to be a mental battle. Don't let him give up or quit fighting. Give him every reason to live. Right now, we've given him something to keep him sedated. That doesn't mean he's not aware of your presence or that he doesn't know what you're saying. Stay positive. I'll give you a few minutes with him."

Celine's stomach did flip-flops and her head began to spin. For hours, she convinced herself that Frank had only minor injuries. This was more than she was prepared to face. Had she just lost her chance at happiness?

She followed the doctor down the corridor, through several sets of doors, and into a neurological trauma unit. There, behind a glass wall, was Frank. Several monitors surrounded the head of his bed and a ventilator kept him breathing. Seeing him like that sent tears to her eyes. "May I touch him?"

"Yes. Just be careful of all the equipment."

She stood next to the bed and took his hand in hers. "Frank, it's Celine. I love you."

Commotion behind her caused her to turn around. Two people had entered the unit, and it didn't take her a split second to realize that the man was Frank's father. Frank was the spitting image of the man, except younger. The woman, she assumed, was Frank's mother.

She turned back to Frank. She squeezed his hand and she could have sworn he squeezed back. Leaning down, she lifted his hand a few inches from the bed and kissed his fingers. "They don't want me to stay here very long. They want you to rest. You better do as they say, because I want you out of here. Besides, you promised you'd take me to the apple orchard."

She reached up and pushed a lock of hair from his forehead. "You are so handsome. How did I get so lucky?"

More noise and raised voices behind her made her realize that she needed to get out of the room. "Your parents are here. I need to leave. They want to see you, too." She held his hand in both of hers, kissed his fingers one more time, and watched for any reaction, but saw none. "I love you. Don't forget that. I love you."

She stepped out of the glass-fronted cubical and walked to the far end of the nurses' station. "When can I see him again?"

The nurse looked up from her monitor and handed Celine a small postcard. "Visitation hours are on here. Do we have your phone number?"

"I gave it to someone downstairs when they

wanted information. I didn't have insurance information." She looked up at the parents, who seem to be staring at her. "Try asking his father."

"Thank you, Mrs. Cresson. I'll suggest that they stop by the registration office. Are you staying in town?"

"No. I'll go home and be back in the morning."

Celine nodded acknowledgment to Frank's parents as she passed them on her way out of the unit. She knew it was not the time or place to talk to them.

She got into her car and found a fast food restaurant. Her favorite place was always closed on Sundays, but most all of them did have some healthier alternatives. She pulled into one, read the drive through menu, and chose the seasonal salad with a side of yogurt. Then she topped it with a cup of coffee. Part of her wanted to cry, not eat, but she had a long drive home, and she knew she had to keep herself pulled together for Frank's sake. She could cry when she was home.

The following morning, she returned to the hospital and brought her laptop with her. She could only see Frank for a few minutes every couple of hours. She had to work. She could go on the company's website and do what she needed to do, only taking a break long enough to see Frank.

Tuesday afternoon, she called Crabby's and informed them that she would need a few days off, as she was keeping vigil at Frank's side. Crabby wasn't very happy, but after working there for years and never missing time, Crabby knew not to chastise her for missing work.

It was late Tuesday evening when Frank's parents entered the waiting room where she sat. It was Frank's father who verbally accosted her, demanding to know who she was, and what she was doing there.

She plastered the sweetest smile she could muster on her face and introduced herself as Celine. Then waited. Many times in her father's life, he had to deal with authorities. He had warned her to say as little as possible. 'Only answer what you absolutely must.' His words played in her head.

It was Frank's mother who seemed to go off in a tirade, demanding to know who Celine was.

"I'm his wife." She turned back to her computer. It was all she could do to hold her ground and not be baited.

"My son is not married."

Celine looked up and waited for a moment. "Which one of you is a lawyer?"

Frank's mother answered, "We both are."

"Will one of you be handling his case?"

Frank's father answered, "Actually, our firm will. Why?"

"I've been saving this for him, knowing that someone would be looking for revenge." She scrolled through the phone numbers. "Is this you?" She held the phone screen so that Frank's father could see it.

"Yes."

Celine pressed a few buttons. As soon as she had the man's email address, she sent a copy of the accident video to his father, knowing full well that Frank had referenced her as his wife. Celine knew it was no different than being in the seventh grade and having that first puppy crush. Except she and Frank were no longer children. She mentally crossed her fingers and hoped that the little ploy would work.

Wednesday, Frank's father left, leaving Frank's mother to stay with her son.

By Thursday afternoon, Celine knew that she was going to have to do more if she was going to convince his family that she was Frank's wife. She left early Thursday evening, and when she returned to her apartment, she searched the envelope the paramedics had handed her. She grabbed the ring of keys and went to the docks. It took her a moment to find the key that would give her access to the boat.

Once inside the yacht, she gathered all of Frank's

belongings and took them to her place. She put his clothes in her closet, hung his coats with hers, and added his razor and other things to her bathroom cabinet. It looked as though he'd been living there with her.

And she cleaned the second bedroom and made it very presentable.

That night, she climbed into bed and imagined him there beside her. She could feel his arms around her, feel his breath in her ear, and her body warmed at the thought. Then reality sent her into tears. *Oh, Frank, why? Why did this have to happen?*

Friday morning, she was back at the hospital, this time she didn't have billing to occupy her time. She pulled out her e-reader and tried to read a book, but her ability to concentrate was lacking. Frank's mother walked into the waiting room. Celine decided that she had to extend an olive branch to the woman, as the mental anguish of seeing her son lying there was taking a toll. Each passing day made the woman look more ashen and the circles under her eyes were getting darker.

Celine attempted a smile. "The doctors seem very hopeful. We just have to ride this out."

Frank's mother frowned. "I doubt that you understand, but that's my son lying there."

"And he's the love of my life. I never dreamed that I would find someone so wonderful, so sweet, so kind... Someone who would love me the way he loves me." She stared at Frank's mother. The woman didn't resemble her son at all. She was tall and very slender. But Celine knew she had to do everything in her power to make Frank's mother believe that Celine and Frank were actually married. Celine asked, "Would you like to come home with me? We've been staying in my apartment while he was waiting for the house."

"With you?"

"Yes. When my mother and father moved away, they split the house into two apartments. I took the upstairs and they rented out the bottom floor. It was a compromise, because I wanted to stay in Mariner's Cove."

"You're inviting me to stay in your apartment?"

"Yes, why not? Certainly living with me has to be better than staying in a hotel. Besides, it will give us a chance to get to know each other. I know you must be very special to have raised such a wonderful son." Celine waited for Frank's mother to answer. It was as though she could watch the gears turning in the woman's head.

"Maybe it would be better. Where do you live?"

"Mariner's Cove is about an hour from here."

Another long pause filled the air, as Celine patiently waited for Frank's mother to decide.

Two weeks turned into three, and Celine knew she had to go back to work for Crabby. She couldn't exist on just her pay from the lab company. She needed more.

November came roaring in, cold and wet. The color in the trees had faded and brown leaves covered the earth. As the temperatures outside turned cooler, Iris Cresson slowly warmed, and Celine discovered that she actually liked the woman.

Several times when Frank was scheduled for tests and various scans, Iris Cresson took a little time and insisted that she and Celine go shopping. Celine remembered shopping with her own mother. Shopping with Iris was different. She was determined to make sure that Celine was dressed in only the best. Whereas Celine's mother pinched pennies, making Celine decide that Iris had probably never had any financial restraints on her.

It was after one of their little forays to a local shopping area that they returned to the hospital and to a waiting doctor, who smiled for a change.

"He's regaining consciousness. The swelling is gone. He needs to completely wake up."

Celine went to Frank and, as always, she took his hand in hers and kissed his fingers. "I love you, Frank. The doctor says we are waiting for you to wake up. He wants you to wake up. I want you to wake up. Open your eyes, Frank."

She held his hand in hers and again, she could've sworn he squeezed her hand. "I want you, Frank. I love you. I want you back with me. I love you, my darling."

This time, he squeezed back. There was no question.

She pushed the nurses' button as she squeezed his hand again. "Open your eyes, Frank. I know you're awake, but you have to open your eyes."

There was a slight flutter to his golden-brown lashes, but his eyes didn't open.

"Try again. You can do it."

A nurse had joined her and was on the far side of the bed. "Open your eyes, Frank." Several monitors beeped as the nurse made adjustments. "We know you are awake. The doctor will be here in just a few minutes. He's going to want to talk to you."

✻

A groggy feeling swept through Frank's system. He wanted to roll over and sleep away the worst hangover of his life, but someone was calling his name.

"Frank, you're in the hospital. You've been in a motorcycle accident. You must wake up and talk to the doctor." The voice sounded like his mother's.

He tried to search his memory, but it was empty. *It's a dream. The accident on the motorcycle was years ago. I was still in college.*

"Open your eyes, Frank. I love you."

He moved both his legs. *No pain. Not broke.*

A man's voice was asking him something.

Light shined into his eyes. He managed to mumble, "Stop that."

"Then open your eyes."

His bed rose and pulled him into a sitting position. He opened his eyes. "Too much light."

Immediately lights in the room dimmed. *This is some sort of a bad dream.*

"Welcome back. Can you tell me your name?"

Name? My name, um, name... Panic spread through him as he tried to remember. "F-f-f... F-f-f." It was too difficult. He wanted to go back to sleep. "What was the question?"

The doctor asked him again, "Do you remember

your name?"

A female, standing someplace behind the doctor huffed. "This is ridiculous. Frank, stop playing games and tell the doctor your name."

It took him a minute to focus. *Mom?* "Frank Cresson. Franklin Elliot Cresson."

"Hi, Frank. I've missed you."

He had no clue as to whom she was, but she was beautiful. She lightly caressed his feet like a lover.

The doctor asked more questions, half of which he couldn't answer. He could remember his birthday and where he worked. His mouth was dry. "Coffee?"

The pretty woman at his feet offered to bring him a cup, and then vanished out the door. He hoped she'd come back, because he didn't know her name.

The doctor was asking him to follow his finger, except he kept making his finger vanish. He shined the flashlight into his eyes, which sent a sharp pain deep into his head. "Please, stop. When you do that it feels as though you're stabbing me in the eyes."

The doctor placed something over his one eye. "Now tell me what you see."

"Nothing."

The doctor did several more things and slowly it began to sink in that he had no vision on one side.

"Am I blind?"

"No. I believe you have some temporary vision loss in your right eye. You've had a severe head trauma and it may take a while before your vision returns. But the eye itself appears to be healthy."

The doctor continued to talk while he poked and prodded. But when the beautiful young woman returned, Frank's heart soared.

"Here's your coffee." She handed him the Styrofoam cup.

He looked at it and managed to sip it. Black and sweet, it was the way he liked it, except it was lousy coffee. The nurse had moved away and now his beautiful maiden stood beside his bed. She smiled at him and he smiled back, but he had no idea who she was. A long French braid swirled her head, fell over her shoulder, and ended someplace near her waist. He would've called it dark brown, except even in the low light it had golden red highlights.

The doctor continued to ask questions, some of which Frank couldn't answer. A feeling of agitation settled into his gut. He could vaguely remember coming to Mariner's Cove and being on the yacht, but anything beyond that was lost.

"It's common to not remember the accident or even a day or two before the accident. In the case of severe trauma, the body goes into survival mode. The brain concentrates on keeping the heart and lungs operational. Memory seems to be a superfluous function. This amnesia is actually quite common. In fact, most people assume amnesia is going to wipe out their entire life and erase every memory that they ever had. That is extremely rare. But what you are experiencing is quite common after a head injury. You'll probably never remember the actual accident or even the hours leading up to it. As I said, memory is an unnecessary function when the body is under tremendous duress."

The doctor came around to where the young woman was standing. He put his hand on her shoulder as he spoke. "Celine, we're going to set your husband up with another CAT scan this evening, and I'll send the therapist here to work with him. In the meantime, I want you to stay with your husband and make sure he does not go back to sleep." The doctor turned to Frank's mother. "Why don't you bring your daughter-in-law some dinner so that she can stay with him?"

Huh? Frank looked at the young woman and then at his mother. He must've lost more than a few days. "I'm married?"

Celine giggled as she took his hand in hers and brought his fingers to her lips.

The feeling of love washed through him. It was familiar, warm, and comforting. Almost as though the feeling had blanketed him for a long time, but he had no memory of her or of being married. He looked at his mother and asked if he could have a few moments alone with Celine.

His mom huffed and left the room. Demanding, no matter what he did, it was never good enough, never perfect, never up to her standards. The love-hate relationship he had with his parents lingered in his mom's wake. From the time he was a small boy, if a report card had a C, it should've been a B. And if it was a B, then why didn't he have an A. The same demands were placed on him when he started working for the family law firm. No matter what it was, it was never good enough. He was sick of trying to please. He remembered running away to Mariner's Cove. It wasn't practicing law that he disliked - it was practicing law with his impossible family, and never being acknowledged for doing well.

He looked at Celine and whispered, "Who are you?"

Chapter 3

*P*anic rushed through Celine like iced water. She didn't want to lie, but she had to somehow help Frank remember the feelings he had for her. For over three long, grueling weeks, she had managed to keep up the farce of being Frank's wife. She didn't want to ruin everything. "Celine Colburn Cresson. You said I was the love of your life."

"We're married?"

"It's a long story. I'll tell you about it when you get out of here."

"I don't remember." He smiled. "But I obviously have great taste when it comes to women, because you are as beautiful as an angel."

"I'm not so sure about being angel, but thank you

for the compliment. I can't imagine being more in love or finding anyone as wonderful as you."

He grabbed her hand and looked at the rings on her finger. "Did I give these to you?"

"Not exactly. They were my grandmother's set."

"So there's some sort of sentimental value to them?"

"Yes. I had no desire for some humongous diamond when these came with such fond memories."

He looked at her as if he could see clear into her soul. "Kiss me?"

Carefully avoiding all the wires and tubes that emanated from his body, she placed her hands on his shoulders and touched her lips to his.

He enveloped her with one arm as his other hand captured her breast.

Part of her exploded into flame as another part felt as though it was dissolving into a hot liquid puddle. Her lips traveled across his whiskered cheek to his ear, where she whispered, "I love you, Frank, I really do love you with all my heart."

"Part of me is angry that I've missed something. I don't remember you, and I certainly don't remember falling in love, but I think I'm going to have fun falling in love with you a second time."

"Then I hope I don't disappoint you."

"I won't hold you to marriage. We'll take it one step at a time." He fingered her long braid. "You've been here with me haven't you? It's as if I remember the love that we shared, but I can't remember you."

⁂

Still minus the sight in his right eye and some weakness on his right side, Frank was allowed to go home. Except home was not back to his old apartment or to the yacht, it was to Celine's apartment. Part of him wanted his mother to leave and to stay out of his life, but he knew that she loved him, and in her own way, she wanted what was best for him. Except her ideas for him were never his.

That night he crawled into the bed he shared with Celine. He had no memory of ever sleeping with her, yet part of him was thrilled. Even though he wanted to make love to her, he was exhausted. He wrapped his arms around her as his head touched the pillow and his eyes closed.

Fortunately the following morning, his mom left. Part of him breathed a sigh of relief as he said goodbye. His whole life had been colored by his mother's domineering personality and he was tired of it. He had Celine, yet she was a stranger.

Celine was busy at her computer and he wondered what she was doing. He stood over her shoulder and looked at the computer screen. Even watching her gave no real clue to what she was typing.

She stopped and smiled at him. "It's how I make my living. Four days a week, I spend six or more hours a day billing patients."

"I'm familiar with the company. Have you always done this?"

"Yes. I got lucky. Eight years ago, I stumbled into this job after taking classes on medical billing. It's been perfect for me."

"If we're married, why are you working?"

"Because I have bills to pay." Her fingers clicked over the keyboard.

He slumped into a chair and looked around the apartment. There was nothing special about it, nothing wonderful, exciting, or beautiful. Various styles of furniture had been combined and painted a pale yellow. Two gold wingback chairs sat opposite a gold and brown printed loveseat. A few cheap prints hung on the walls. It wasn't bad, but it wasn't great. It reminded him of a student's first apartment. "How long was I here before the accident?"

"I can't talk to you and do my work, too."

Frank stood up and poured himself another cup of coffee. There was no memory of any of this, nothing, totally blank. "Celine, please stop. We need to talk."

✳

Celine could feel her stomach tightening. The time had come to tell him the truth. Taking a deep breath she responded, "Please give me a few moments to finish what I'm doing, and I'll tell you everything."

She shut down her computer, grabbed a fresh cup of coffee, and sat opposite Frank on the little loveseat. Her insides quaked as she tried to find the right words. It'd taken everything she had to avoid lying beyond saying that she was Frank's wife. Even with Frank's mother staying in her tiny apartment, she had still managed to keep up the charade. She had to tell him the truth.

Frank was not the man she first met. Still blind in his right eye, she wasn't certain he'd ever recover. His entire right side was weaker than his left. Yet somehow, she knew that Frank was still the most fabulous man she had ever met. Words formed and dissipated in her mind. She had to tell him, even if he hated her for it.

Sucking in a deep breath, she closed her eyes for a moment. "What do you want to know?"

"Everything. I have no memory of you, none." He reached over and pulled her to his lap. His finger stroked her cheek.

She didn't want to lie. She wanted to tell the truth, but at this point, fear of losing him kept her from uttering the necessary words. Tears slipped from the corners of her eyes. She tried to push them away, but more followed.

"Ah, don't cry, baby. At least you have your memories. I'm missing days." He ran his fingers down her neck, and then cupped her breast. "I can see why I've fallen in love with you. You're beautiful. But I don't even remember how I met you. In fact, I've almost worried what I might've done. I can remember coming up here, I can remember living on the yacht, and someplace in the deep recesses of my mind, I remember I wanted to buy a house."

"You did, well, almost. You signed the papers for it."

"I did?"

She pushed up and off him and the sofa. In the closet, in her bedroom, she had a plastic container where she had stashed all of what she considered to be his personal papers. Grabbing the container, she took it back and handed it to him. Then she went into the kitchen and retrieved his cell phone. "I think you will find all of your answers."

She went back to her bedroom and threw herself across her bed. Tears, along with emotions that she had tried so hard to tamp down for weeks, rose like an angry geyser inside of her. Her little white lie that allowed her access to him in the hospital had spilled into his family, and now played with his already compromised memory. Once the truth was discovered, he would hate her. The thrill of discovering his feelings had matched hers, instantly fell like burning embers into her guts. She had ruined everything. All she could do was wait for his wrath.

Frank looked over the paperwork. Everything appeared to be there, including the contract on the house. The only thing he couldn't find was a copy of the marriage license. An official copy from the state often took as much as six weeks, but there was always something left with the bridal couple. *Maybe she has it.*

The title for his cycle was mixed into his papers. He wondered where that cycle was, and if there was anything left of it.

He picked up his phone and looked through it. There were text messages. He remembered those. He went back to the papers and found the accident report. It didn't seem real. It was as though the whole thing happened to someone else. Nothing. Not a shred of memory. That Sunday was totally gone, as was Thursday, Friday, and Saturday leading up to that day.

Huh? How do I lose four days and a wife? How did I gain a wife in four days?

He put the papers down and closed the box. Then he looked through his phone messages. Swiping the screen, he looked at the photo app. He went back to the box and found the tiny black box. *My helmet cam. Oh please tell me I was wearing it.*

He found a USB cord and hooked it to his cam. It took a minute to sort to what he thought was the video.

It started with him on the yacht. He looked at his smiling face and listened. "Today I'm taking Mrs. Franklin Cresson for a ride. I cannot imagine being more in love than I am with Celine. She is absolutely the perfect wife for me."

He watched the entire thing almost stunned. Backing up the video, he watched the impact over and over. But right before the impact, Celine stood on the far corner of the street. She raised her left hand and waved. He tapped the screen, honed in, and expanded the picture. There were no rings on her finger. *No newlywed female is going to remove her rings.*

He couldn't see himself in any of the video, but for a fraction of a second, he saw his bike skidding along on its side, and he could see Bobby Finch's boat trailer on its side as a small blue sports car flipped several times until it stopped abruptly against what he decided must have been the seawall.

It felt as though he was watching a movie. It wasn't him – he had nothing to do with any of it. He knew he went through Shelby's plate glass window, because he had been told. But the first impact must have sent his helmet cam rolling along in a different direction.

Maybe it was better that he couldn't remember anything. Maybe it gave him a much more objective view of what happened. There was no question in his mind that his dad was gathering as much as he could to begin a suit against the driver of the blue sports car. He would be doing the same if it had been his dad.

He rested his head on the back of the sofa and covered his right eye with his hand. How could he explain that his eye ached like a nagging headache?

The pesky sensation that something wasn't exactly right remained, and he was certain that Celine knew something that she wasn't telling him. The rings played on his mind. He couldn't even imagine being stone drunk and getting married to someone he didn't know. Drugged? He guessed it would be possible, but his wild days were over. He'd often have a beer or two in the evening. But drunk or drugged? *No way.* In his own words, he knew he had fallen in love. *But married?*

He stood and went in search of Celine. He found her asleep across her bed, and it was obvious that she had been crying. He climbed beside her and rubbed her back. Her left hand was tucked near her face. He looked at the rings. They were old, very old. Not a jeweler around would sell such a set without properly polishing them. They were definitely something that Celine had inherited.

What if we're not really married? But why? Why the charade? He mulled that over in his mind. Then he remembered that amid the papers, Celine had accepted his personal effects. *My keys. Access to the yacht.*

There was cash in his wallet. The ATM slip was there. He was certain she'd not taken a single dollar. Everything seemed to be in order. She was working, acting as though she had to make every penny she could.

Deep in the recesses of his mind, he knew she was at the hospital, keeping vigil over him. She lived alone, had a job, and she wasn't stealing from him. *How? Why?* He rolled onto his back and stared at the ceiling.

A four-day romance that ended in marriage and a motorcycle accident? It wasn't the least bit logical. Celine held the missing pieces.

In her sleep, she snuggled to his shoulder and he held her. That prompted his mind to the sexual nature of their relationship. Had he made love to her? Had they used protection? Could she be pregnant with his child? *She fits so perfectly to me as though she's always been here next to me.*

Like a bird tweeting the same song over and over, he mulled over what he knew. And when the scent of food filled his nostrils, he opened his eyes. Celine was long gone from the bed and darkness emanated from the windows. He looked at the small clock in her room and realized he had slept for more than two hours. He got up and joined her in the kitchen.

"Celine, I need some answers. I'm a lawyer. I'm used to asking questions and being given truthful responses."

She shrugged. "Not a problem. What would you like to know?"

He studied her movements. They were fluid and soft. "Where did we meet?"

"Crabby's. It's a little restaurant by the harbor. I work there on Thursday, Friday, and Saturday nights." She took a glass pan from the oven and placed it in the center of the table on a small piece of towel.

He wasn't certain, but it looked as though it contained stuffed pork chops. But whatever it was, it smelled delicious. She washed her hands, tossed a salad, and then placed a bowl of applesauce on the table.

"Dinner is ready."

He held a chair for her and then took the one on the opposite side of the table. Her china was old but beautiful, and her silverware appeared to be every bit as old. Just from the weight and sheen, he knew it was solid silver and worth a fortune for someone like her.

She put a small amount of salad on a pressed glass

plate and then passed him the bowl.

Everything was plain and simple, yet tasted delicious. "This is a real treat. Are you trying to spoil me?"

She giggled. "I'm only trying to feed my husband without poisoning him."

"Something tells me you're probably a very good cook."

"I try. My mom taught me."

He stabbed a forkful of salad and then held it midair. "When did we first meet?"

"On a Thursday. Except we were so busy because the restaurant was shorthanded, I barely had time to say hello."

"*We* were so busy? Who *is* we?"

"Crabby's Pot House. I'm a waitress there. And for the record, you came on to me."

"And what about Friday?"

"Same problem."

"Okay, that brings us to Saturday. What happened on Saturday?"

"You spotted me as I ran errands and invited me on your yacht, and then you took me out to see the house. I had to be work before five."

"What house?"

"The house you are buying. Except it had been

owned by a guy who was into kink. I don't know if you remember that."

"I remember the house, and I saw where I signed the contract. Although I have no memory of doing that." He speared another bite of salad. "And Sunday morning, what did we do?"

"I went to the yacht and had coffee with you. That's when you decided that we needed to go for a ride."

"Except we never left Mariner's Cove, did we?"

He watched her swallow before she answered, "No."

"We never had some wild, whirlwind romance, did we?"

She shook her head, as tears slipped over her cheeks.

"Turn off the waterworks. Just tell me why you've told everyone we are married."

She grimaced and more tears slipped down her cheeks. She wiped them away with her napkin, but they continued to fall.

"I'm not going to sit here and watch you cry. There are no reasons for tears. A simple explanation is all I'm asking."

She sniffled. "Because I knew that they would never let me near you in the hospital, because I wasn't your wife. It was a little white lie, but it grew when your family came."

"Why didn't you tell my mom that we weren't really married and you had told the hospital that you were my wife so you could stay with me?"

She raised her shoulders and let them drop. "At first, I didn't trust her. I figured she'd tell the hospital and then I wouldn't be allowed to see you."

That caused him to laugh. "I don't always trust her, and she's my mom. And you are right, she probably would have told the hospital."

Celine sniffled again. "But when I got to know her, she was so sweet. She loves you so much. She fussed the whole time about what a horrible mother she had been because she worked instead of staying home with you."

"And she's very protective of me to the point of... Never mind."

Tugging at the shoulder of her shirt, she continued. "She kept wanting to buy me clothes – expensive clothes! I kept telling her I had more than enough."

"That's my mom."

"Well, I offered to pay her but she said no, because I was family." Another wave of tears spilled down her cheeks. "I didn't take a penny from you. But I didn't know how to stop her. If you get her to tell you how much I owe her, I'll get a cash advance on my credit card and pay her back."

He shook his head and took a bite of his chop. "Don't worry about it. For a few weeks, she had the daughter she never had."

She swiped away her tears. "I'm sorry."

"Explain why didn't you tell me the truth."

"I was scared. I knew you'd be furious with me and..." She grimaced again. "I'd fallen in love with you. I know it's stupid. No one falls in love without actually knowing a person. But when I saw the video on the phone, I knew you had those same feelings." More tears flowed. "I wanted us to have a chance." She flew from the table.

Frank put his elbows on the table and rested his head in his hands. Part of him understood what she had done and why, but there was this tiny little niggling spot that was still angry over the deceit that had extended to his family. Maybe he was at the same crossroad, but for a different reason. He wasn't ready to let go of Celine. She hadn't really done anything wrong. In her own way, she had created a buffer around him.

If she hadn't, he'd be coping with his mom, who would have hovered over him as though he were a little boy with a sore throat who'd stayed home from school.

He didn't remember the weeks he'd spent in the hospital, but in the deep recesses of his mind, he knew he was loved. He looked at his hands as though he should know something, but his hands were fine. He'd spend a few weeks in therapy until he'd rebuild his strength on that side. And with a little luck, his sight in his right eye would return. He figured this would be easy compared to that fateful year in college when he shattered his leg in the motocross accident.

He wanted to go to Celine and tell her that everything was going to be okay, but he wasn't certain it would. Maybe he wanted them to have a chance.

He pushed his chair back and stood. She was lying on her bed with her back to him. He sat next to her and tried to gather his thoughts into something comprehensible. "Celine, I wasn't expecting to wake up married." A small chuckle rose up his throat. "That was a serious shock. But I couldn't have asked for a better wife." He ran his hand across her shoulder and down her arm. "Except, we need to put an end to the charade."

He leaned over and kissed her head. "I'd like to suggest that we start over, but maybe it's too late for that. If I go back to the yacht that will make Brook think that we've had some sort of lover's quarrel, which will go straight back to my family. On the other hand, I shouldn't be sleeping with you. I'm going to presume that we hadn't progressed to that level."

He watched what he thought might have been another sniffle and he wished she would put an end to the tears.

"We did sleep together last night." Her voice was mumbled by her pillow.

"And the operative word in that sentence is sleep. Let's try to give this relationship a chance. If it doesn't work out, we'll have to file for a fake divorce."

She rolled over and grinned at him. "You'd divorce me after I put up with your mom for three weeks?"

"Too bad. It's your fault that you were nice to her and that you lied."

"Do you really mean it when you said that you'll give us a chance?"

❧

A few days later, Celine picked up her phone and was surprised to hear from Frank's mom. Celine tried hard to sound upbeat, but inside she could feel her stomach trembling. "Thanksgiving? Oh, I'll have to ask Frank. He's at therapy. May I call you back?"

She got off the phone as quickly as she could. *Oh, yes. I can see it now. We get to be the happy couple for his family.*

Quickly she changed into her waitress uniform. She knew darn well that Crabby wouldn't be thrilled with her taking off over the holiday. It was bad enough when she took off for three weeks, but to ask off for Thanksgiving? She knew he'd be furious with her. That was a limited dinner menu consisting of a traditional New England feast. People had two choices, seafood or no seafood. People came for miles for his smoked turkey with oyster dressing.

She barely had time to think. She had to pick up Frank, and then be at work.

Frank smiled broadly as she pulled into the circle by the door to the therapy center. He got into her old car with a grin that wouldn't quit.

She smiled back. "Okay, I know you ate the canary, so tell me what your news is, and then I'll tell you mine."

"I'm off those baby pink weights. They moved me up to the yellow ones. But they told me to keep working at home with soup cans."

"That sounds wonderful!" She pulled onto the

main road and headed back to Mariner's Cove. "You're progressing faster than you thought you would."

"Yes. They are thrilled with me. What's your news?"

She looked over at him for a split second. "You're not going to believe who called me today and expects us for Thanksgiving dinner."

"Um, do I get three guesses?"

"No, just one."

"My mom."

"You got that right. Seems your family is all going to be gathering at your Uncle Archie's house." She signaled a left turn as she approached a red light. "Everyone is looking forward to meeting the bride."

"I'd like to think you're joking, but knowing my mom, this is serious."

"Oh, it's serious, all right. Apparently she's told everyone about me."

"And we are expected to arrive when?"

"Wednesday evening and we are supposed to stay through the weekend. Crabby is going to have a conniption."

"You could just quit. You don't need to work."

She pulled into the back alley behind the restaurant. "Just in case you've forgotten, we really aren't married. I'm not going to mooch off of you."

Frank came around to her side of the car and opened the door. "Think on this. If we're supposed to stay with my mom and dad, they are going to be expecting us to share a bed."

She smiled up at him. "We're mature adults. I'm certainly capable of staying on my side."

"And you think I'm not?"

She punched in the security code on the back door of the restaurant. "Well you seem to be the one who is more concerned about us sharing a bed."

"We could discuss the concept of friends with perks."

※

Frank didn't trust Celine's little car to make the long trip to his family's home. He rented one.

Celine took one look at the car and the color drained from her face. "You want me to drive that?"

"It's not big. The only thing big about it is the engine."

"I don't care what's under the hood. I'm not used to driving it. Why can't I use my car?"

"Your car has almost three hundred thousand

miles on it. I don't trust it to make the long trip."

She rolled her eyes at him.

Sometimes he wanted to laugh at her and other times, she frustrated him. At the moment, she was frustrating him. "Let's take it for a drive to the house I've bought. It'll give you a chance to get used to driving it before we leave for my family's. Besides I want to see what's going on with the house."

"Fine."

A few minutes later, they were on their way to the house. The drive itself was lovely. Crispy and cool with a bright almost cloudless day, it was the quintessential November day. Brown leaves swirled along the edges of the road. It would've been a perfect day to take the motorcycle. He also knew Celine was petrified of the idea of him riding. He understood her fear, but he had yet to convince her that it was a freak accident. He watched out the passenger window at the passing landscape. Here and there, he could see the ocean in the distance.

When they reached their destination, he was surprised to find several pickup trucks in the driveway, and a huge dumpster sitting beside the house. He opened Celine's driver's door. "It wasn't so bad driving out here was it?"

"No. Maybe I'm just used to my own car."

"Your problem is that you are so used to pinching pennies that you don't know how to spend a few dollars. I'm not saying that's a bad thing." He took her hand in his.

She brought his hand to her lips and kissed his fingers. Wonderful warm feelings flowed through him every time she did it. It was such a small gesture, yet somehow it felt like much, much more.

"Do you realize that Brook was married before?"

"I assumed he was; I know he has a daughter."

"Wife number one knew only how to spend money. No matter what it was, it was never enough. She always wanted something bigger, better, more expensive, or lavish."

Celine looked at him with raised eyebrows. "Brook?"

He nodded. "The complete opposite of Nikki. I don't want a wife that's going to spend money faster than I can make it."

"Well, you've probably already figured out that I'm very careful with my money."

"I don't know what you make or how much you spend. But it's quite apparent that you are very thrifty." He opened the front door to the house.

The entire first floor was gutted. There were no walls, but in several areas there seemed to be posts holding up the ceiling. Sounds of demolition emanated from someplace above them. He called out with no answer, and tried again. That time his call was answered.

A lanky, blue-eyed, blond male came down the stairs. "May I help you?"

"I'm Frank Cresson."

"You're the guy who was in the accident, and the new owner. I'm Mike Silvia." He brushed his hand on his pants before extending it. "We've talked on the phone."

Taking Mike's hand, Frank shook it. "Yes. How's the house coming along?"

"Being we can work, rain or shine, everything is going exactly as planned. But I do think we need to go over a few things. I need to order things such as kitchen cabinets and the counters."

"We can meet next Monday at two o'clock."

"Excellent. Would you like to meet at my office or here?"

Frank looked at Celine, she shrugged and pointed to the floor as she answered, "Here at the house."

"Let's do it here. I want a feel for the space. But shouldn't I have an architect or something to draw up the official plans?"

The man walked across the empty house towards

the back door. There next to the door was tacked a list and a scribbled drawing that Frank had made, and next to them was a very tidy drawing. Mike lifted all three from the wooden stud and brought them to Frank. "Would you like a copy of my drawing?"

Frank looked and smiled. Every idea had been incorporated into the precision drawing. The man before him had done exactly what his good friend, Ken Taylor, did with ideas for motorcycles.

Mike pointed to the walls. "I'm bringing in new insulation. What was here was old and the newer R ratings make the old stuff obsolete. The shakes are in good shape. There are only a few that I feel need to be replaced. You said to make it right."

Frank listened and nodded as though he understood everything the man was saying. The pounding sounds coming from upstairs were giving him a headache.

"I'm going to suggest you change the staircase. The old-style won't match with what you want."

Again, Frank nodded. "I'll let you get back to work. And I'll see you next Monday."

"Thanks. I'll bring everything with me, including a copy of my drawing."

Frank took Celine's hand and they walked outside. "Sorry. Listening to them work is giving me a major headache."

"Think you should go to the ER?"

"No. I'll be fine, but I do get the feeling that I'm going to have problems with noise levels, or at least certain types of noise."

*

The following morning, Celine stretched as she opened her eyes. The sky had lightened from a deep navy blue and appeared to be tinged with lilac. She wasn't ready to get up, but she knew she didn't dare roll over and go back to sleep. She had a long drive ahead of her.

Slipping on her robe and putting her feet into slippers, she padded her way towards the kitchen. As she passed the guest room, she could tell that Frank was still sleeping. It wasn't exactly a snore - more like noisy breathing. She stopped and listened to him. Her heart pounded in her chest. She loved him and she was certain that he loved her. Maybe it was the way he held her hand, or the way he looked at her.

Worry crept through her. Tonight they would be sharing a bed. That first night, when his mom was still at the apartment, had been easy, for he had been exhausted. But would they both be that tired tonight? She knew her feelings, knew that she wanted his arms around her, wanted to touch him, feel his skin against hers, and yet a single passionate kiss would probably unravel the precarious relationship they had built.

She stepped away from his door, into the kitchen, and began making a pot of coffee as she continued to think about the two of them. She didn't want what they had to dissolve into a strictly sexual liaison. Had she reached the point where she was tired of living alone? No, that wasn't it - her life was fine. There was no denying the spark of energy that flowed between them. That crackle and sizzle that warmed every part of her body. Never before had a man elicited such feelings in her. And hadn't her mother always told her when the right man comes along she'd know it?

The thought of the charade that they would play this weekend sent a round of apprehension clear to her toes. They had already practiced what they were going to say if someone asked how they met and when they married. They didn't need some tiny detail tripping them. But she wasn't thrilled with spinning more lies.

She poured a cup of coffee for herself and then decided to pour one for Frank and take it to him. Carrying both cups, she stepped into the room. She put the drinks on his nightstand and sat on the edge of the bed. *So handsome*. She ran her fingers through his hair and then down his arm, before lifting his hand to her lips and kissing his fingers as she had done hundreds of times as he lay in the hospital.

His eyes fluttered open and he smiled. "Good morning. Have I overslept?"

"No. Thought you'd like a cup of coffee."

He sat up and grabbed for his cup. "What did I do to deserve being spoiled like this?"

"Nothing." She looked away for a moment and then returned her gaze to him. "In a way, I wish we really were married. I hate lying."

"You're worried about being with my family?"

She nodded.

"They are people, just like a few million other people. Bank accounts only allow them to spend more." He took another sip of his coffee. "You've heard the expression that they put their pants on the same way - well, it's true. My family isn't perfect. No one is perfect."

"What's with you and your mom?"

He rolled his hand over and held it up. "My parents didn't like my riding motocross. They thought I was supposed to be quiet and studious, more like Brook. By the way, at home, we call him

Ivy, as in the Roman numerals I V, because he's the fourth. He's Archer Brooklyn, the fourth." He waved his hand through the air as if to dismiss everything. "Brook was the perfect son. My world has been motorcycles. That wasn't considered proper. I was supposed to play tennis and golf, except I didn't. I got a thrill out of doing the near impossible, pushing myself to the limits."

She found herself nodding at what he was saying. "I completely understand. When I was growing up my mom used to tell me that I couldn't do things because I was girl."

"And you didn't like that?"

"No."

"What were you supposed to be doing?"

"I don't know - cooking, sewing. They were panic stricken to leave me behind and move away."

"Have you proven anything to yourself or to them?"

She drank what was left in her coffee cup. "I survive without help. When the shower dripped, I went on YouTube and figured out how to fix it. Maybe my life isn't glamorous, but I'm fine with it."

"I think you do very well."

"So do I." She stood. "I need to get ready."

She grabbed a quick shower, dressed, and then

began to pack her things. Frank's mom had bought her a pretty cashmere sweater with a scalloped neckline. It was the nicest thing that she owned, and she figured it was the perfect thing for Thanksgiving dinner with his family.

She didn't own much jewelry and the neckline begged for something special. If only she had something that wasn't clunky. Then she remembered the double strand of pearls from her grandmother. The antique necklace was perfect. She added the tiny 14K gold ball earrings that she'd had since she was a small child.

Satisfied with her choices, she closed her suitcase and went to the kitchen. She searched her refrigerator. Being gone for five days, she needed to use up whatever she could. Three eggs, two slices of bacon, and a few slices of cheese - she made egg sandwiches and added a fruit cup to the meal.

Frank declared it perfect, which pleased her. After their breakfast, he placed their suitcases into the trunk of the car while she washed the dishes and put them away. She thought the mundane chores would help settle the butterflies, but the fluttering in her stomach wouldn't stop. The mix of feelings seemed to build in her, and her hands shook.

Part of her wanted to laugh, because the idea of

them being married was totally crazy. It would've been so much easier if she were merely dating Frank. Catching up with him on the yacht each morning would've been heaven compared to keeping up the sham of marriage. She took a couple of deep breaths, pulled on her coat. "Let the show begin."

The drive to Frank's parents' seemed to take forever. They stopped once for coffee and again for lunch. Several times, she tried to tell herself to relax, but driving on the superhighway with all the traffic totally scared her. Her hands were hurting from gripping the steering wheel and the tension spread across her shoulders, up her neck, around her head, into her forehead. She was certain that Frank would rather have been driving, because he managed to bark orders at her seemingly every two seconds.

"Need to be in the left lane." A few minutes later, he was telling her to get into the right lane.

"Would you rather I pulled over and allowed you to drive?"

"Yes. I'd rather drive. You know darn well the doctor won't let me."

"Other than giving me instructions on how to get there, I'd appreciate it if you allowed me to just drive."

Twice she was forced to slow to a crawl, taking

almost twenty minutes to barely move four miles. She knew by the time they arrived at his parents' home, she'd be a frazzled wreck. But as they rode through the town and into a fabulous neighborhood, the nervous edge of driving had already begun to wane.

Frank instructed her to turn left and she pulled to a stop in front of a set of gates. She put the code he'd given her into the little unit, and slowly the gates yawned open.

She drove down the long driveway and a beautiful home came into view. The nervousness of driving was instantly replaced with the nervousness of seeing his family. His father had only spent a few hours at the hospital and then had returned to New York. It was hardly enough time to know the man. But Frank's mom had stayed with her in her tiny apartment. Celine took a deep breath and then slowly exhaled. *I'm going to be fine, and I'm going to get through this.*

She had no sooner put the car in park when Frank's mom and dad appeared on the front porch. Frank came around and opened Celine's door. She tried to smile but she wasn't certain she had succeeded. Her anxiety took over and pounded her as though she were a small pebble that had been tossed into the surf.

Iris Cresson hugged her son. "I'm so thrilled you came. I've been so worried about you." Iris turned and enveloped Celine in a warm embrace. "This is going to be so exciting. I can't wait to show off my new daughter-in-law to the entire family and all our friends."

Celine gulped.

Chapter 4

*F*rank took Celine to what had once been his bedroom. Painted in what could only be described as a faded robin-egg blue, the room was large and lovely. Frank admitted it was not what he had wanted as a child. This was a sophisticated version of that room. Still, it was a room that they were being forced to share, and the large king-sized bed sent a cold shiver down her back. She unpacked her things and hung her clothes in the closet, where the wrinkles would fall from the woolen articles.

She had barely finished putting everything away when Iris Cresson appeared in the doorway. "Do you need anything?"

Celine smiled "No thank you. I think we have

everything."

"Wonderful. Come join us downstairs. I have a light meal planned, and then we're going to my youngest sister's house for the rest of the evening. She and her husband can't wait to meet you."

Another round of panic flowed through Celine. "What's the dress code?"

"Tonight it is casual. Tomorrow will be casually suitable for an important family dinner."

Celine nodded at her pretend mother-in-law and tried to act as normal as possible. "Wonderful! I'm looking forward to it."

As soon as the woman left, Celine changed into something a little nicer for dinner, as she wasn't certain exactly what casual meant.

When she emerged from the bathroom, Frank looked at her and grinned. "You look good enough to eat."

"I guess I should take that as a compliment."

He squinted his left eye closed and looked through the right. "I can't exactly see, but I'm seeing something. It's like trying to see through a semi-opaque screen."

"That's wonderful!" She went to him and gazed into his face. "Can you see me, now?"

He shook his head. "Not really, but I can tell that

you're here. It's like... I'm seeing something."

She placed her hands on his chest. "That's the best news you've had in days."

"It gives me hope." He took her hand and led her downstairs.

The house was filled with beautiful antique furniture. Heavy oriental rugs covered plank floors and delicate china knickknacks sat by brass candlestick lamps. The living room was empty of people when they entered. The décor was softer than the rest of the house. Off-white patterned, silk-covered sofas and chairs begged to swaddle the occupant in downy comfort. Colorful Tiffany lamps and Impressionist paintings added counterpoints to the otherwise neutral room.

"Here." Frank led her to the sofa and tucked her next to him.

"This place is unreal. You grew up in this house?" She was still trying to take in all the things in the room.

He nodded.

"Where did you play?"

"Wherever I wanted." He grinned at her.

"You played in here?"

"Oh, there's more than a few scratches on the furniture from me. I'm respons--"

"There you are!" Frank's father came into the room. "And our lovely Celine."

Frank stood and greeted his father. A moment later, Frank's mother joined them, carrying a tray filled with little hors d'oeuvres.

"Tonight is simple. Vanessa wanted to take off early today so she could prepare her family's meal."

Frank nudged Celine and whispered, "That's our cook."

"We're going to have steaks on the grill. Vanessa made the other things ahead of time."

Celine eyed the tray of food and wanted to try one of everything. She just didn't want to be the first person to reach for it.

✳

Frank leaned forward, took a small plate and handed it to Celine. As he filled his plate, Celine put one of everything on hers, and his dad joined them. Then his father began to talk about the accident. Frank's father was already preparing the suit against the driver of the blue car, and was merely awaiting Frank's signature before proceeding.

Frank laughed. "There is nothing quite like hitting

a member of the largest personal injury law firm."

Frank's mother clapped her hands together and held them to her chest. "Oh, darling, does this mean you'll be coming back to the firm?"

Frank raised one shoulder and let it drop as he stuffed a little caviar-laden canapé into his mouth and then refilled his little plate. "I haven't decided what I'm going to do. I'm not going to work elsewhere. When I said I wanted some time off, I meant it. I was thinking of working with Ken Taylor for a few months. He could use the help. But," he smiled at Celine, "since I have my beautiful wife, I haven't decided what I want to do or where I want to live."

"And you bought a house on the water," Frank's mother said. "I think it's a lovely idea to have your own little summer home. It will give you two a nice retreat."

"I was thinking of living there year-round."

Frank's father cleared his throat. "Then you're going with Ivy?"

"I really have not discussed it with him, and I don't want to have that conversation until I am certain what I want to do."

"Well, certainly you won't throw all your education out the window and forget that you're a lawyer." His mother looked indignant.

"No, Mom. I'm not going to throw away everything. I'm only looking for something more exciting than what these last few years have been."

Frank's father stood. "We have the whole weekend to discuss this. For now, we need to grill the steaks."

Frank picked up the tray of hors d'oeuvres and carried it to a beautiful sun porch that protruded off the back of the house. His mother had already set the table. To her, this was a picnic. A bottle of red wine had been opened and was being allowed to breathe. The center of the table was filled with a flower arrangement of colorful fall leaves made of silk and a variety of cut mums. But what surprised him, was the table had been set for eight.

His mother scurried away to answer a phone.

When she returned, Frank asked, "Mom, who else is coming?"

"I invited your Uncle Lloyd and Aunt Kathy. I know how much they want to meet Celine."

Frank gulped. His Uncle Lloyd was his mother's younger brother and a partner. He looked at Celine. "Seems you'll be meeting all the Brooklyns."

His mom quickly responded, "Your Aunt Michelle and Uncle Michael will also be coming to dinner. I just talked to them on the phone. After dinner, we're all going to their house for dessert." She turned to Celine. "Aunt Michelle is my youngest sister, and she married Michael Fields. We're all family in the firm."

Celine nodded as though she understood everything.

Frank was certain that his mom had probably talked to Celine about all the members of the family. He helped his father start the grill and found a plate with eight filet mignons waiting in the refrigerator. He sensed it was going to be a long night.

He watched Celine. Well mannered, she didn't make a single mistake through the meal. And when everyone was done eating, she quietly began to gather the dishes. He knew what she was doing, and he joined her. Between the two of them, and in a matter of minutes, they had the kitchen in perfect order. Then they rejoined the family.

Aunt Michelle raised her eyebrows. "And what were our newlyweds doing?"

Frank chuckled. "We just saved Mom from worrying about the kitchen."

Celine was positively the perfect wife. His parents were thrilled with her, and so were his aunts and uncles. And when Celine was asked about her background, she had responded in such a way that they approved and never questioned beyond what she had said. But from the little bit Celine had told him, he knew the family had struggled until her dad's recent promotion. They were members of the working class, average people with average jobs, scraping by on a lousy paycheck.

When Frank thought about it, his own family wasn't much different than other families, except his family had money. Money to buy things and money to live well, but under the façade that money provided, they were average people. His mother's siblings somehow managed to get along, but the cousins didn't. That's what drove Brook to Mariner's Cove, and took the joy out of winning from Frank. He didn't want to reach the point of being so angry that he couldn't stand going to work. Brook's situation was more personal because it involved a cousin and his ex-wife. But that previous marriage had already been strained by her spending.

Frank looked at Celine and smiled. She was careful with money and he figured she always would be. He couldn't imagine her not watching every penny.

After dinner, everyone shifted to his aunt and uncle's house for dessert and coffee. If the evening had been a test, Celine passed with a perfect score. Each family member appeared to be falling madly in love with her.

But there was one problem left to solve that evening, and that was sharing a bed with her. And he wasn't certain he'd be able to keep up his end of the agreement.

✳

Celine shuddered as she entered the bedroom. Nervous tension had skimmed her body the entire evening as her little white lie about being married had dug a deep trench within Frank's family. But she was facing her biggest one. Sharing the bed with Frank wasn't going to be easy.

"Celine, why don't you use the bathroom first? When you're done, I'll take a quick shower."

She nodded in his direction, found her pajamas and robe, and scurried to the privacy of the bathroom. She pulled her hair into a clip and took a quick shower. Her pajamas were cute, but far from sexy. She put her robe over them, gathered up her clothing, took a deep breath, and left the bathroom.

While she waited for Frank to return, she paced. The tired feeling that bore down on her throughout the evening somehow escaped her. In her mind, there was a tennis match. One side of her knew she needed to remain strong and celibate, but the other side of her wanted to feel his arms around her, his kisses on her neck, to feel him take her as a man would take his wife.

She listened to him turn off the water and heard the sound of his electric razor. She waited. When he emerged from the bathroom, he looked wonderful. He wore a pair of plaid navy blue and burgundy pajama bottoms and a navy blue tee shirt. Broad shoulders that tapered to his waist sent a warm surge of yearning through her that settled into her lower abdomen. The sensation was delicious.

Riveted in place by her feelings, she stared at him.

The edges of his lips curled upwards.

That tiny smile that he wore so often she found endearing.

"I'm not going to molest you, Celine. I know you're concerned. Discussing it on the drive down is one thing and putting it into practice is another." He rolled his hands over palms up. "Not saying I wouldn't enjoy it, but I promised that I'd stay on my side of the bed. I am a gentleman." He pulled back the covers on the bed. "Ready?"

Hesitantly she sat on the far side, slipped her feet under the covers, and turned her back to Frank as she pulled the covers up over her shoulder. She lay motionless, listening to his sounds. The urge to put her head on that soft spot by his shoulder was overwhelming. His fresh from the shower scent filled her lungs with each breath. She fisted her hands to keep from touching him.

She felt the bed move and heard him roll over. She rolled towards the center, thinking she'd be facing his back, instead he was on his stomach. Gingerly she placed her hand on his back and a little moan could be heard coming from Frank.

"I know. I feel the same way." She patted his shoulder blade.

He leaned up and turned to her. "Good. I don't feel so rotten."

"Well, it's nice to know I'm not alone in my feelings."

"Now what?"

She punched at her pillow. "We fight it or we decide to become friends with perks."

"Don't dangle that carrot in front of me."

"Why? Certainly you have a condom on you."

"Do you?"

"No. Why would I have condoms?"

He groaned and rolled so his back was facing her. "Well, neither do I. Go to sleep."

"It's not my fault that you don't have any

condoms."

"Well, we agreed that this was all a front, and if I remember correctly, you said we could do this without any problems."

"Right, blame me for everything."

He sat up and turned to her. "Who got us into this predicament in the first place? Who told my parents we were married? Certainly not me, I was unconscious in the hospital."

She sat up and tucked her legs under her. "Yes. You were, and if I hadn't told the hospital we were married, I would have been banned from seeing you. I felt so horrible. You were coming to pick me up for a fun day of riding when you were hit. I watched that accident, terrified. Why are we rehashing this?"

He blew out a long deep breath. "This is going to be a very long weekend. I'll buy some condoms in the morning so that we have them if we need them. But in the meantime, we need to get some sleep."

Celine nodded. "I don't think morning can get here fast enough."

She slipped under the covers once again, as a gazillion thoughts started to whirl in her mind. Soon Frank's breathing turned into that same rhythm she had listened to for hours in the hospital. But every minute sound had her wide-eyed and staring into the darkness of Frank's old bedroom. Her old house creaked and made weird sounds every time the heater kicked on, and comparatively this place was almost silent.

And when morning came, it seemed as though she hadn't slept at all. Yet she knew she had. Gingerly she sat up and stared at Frank. His one hand lay on his chest and she picked it up, almost out of habit. She threaded her fingers with his and brought that hand to her lips and kissed it.

Frank's eyes flew open. "You used to do that to me in the hospital, didn't you?"

"Do what?"

"Pick my hand up and kiss it."

"Yes. They had you hooked up to so many things that I was afraid to touch you anyplace but on your hand."

"I remember tidbits of things - noises, but not enough of anything to identify the sounds. Yet I remember the wonderful feeling of being loved, and that feeling flowing into me through my hand."

"They told me there are several stages of a coma, sort of like layers. As your brain healed, you progressed through the layers. And towards the end, you were in the lightest stage. At one point, I thought you were actually awake, but you weren't. They said you were reacting to stimuli, which was very positive."

She looked at his hand. It appeared to be twice the size of hers. She remembered when she first saw him. He was a man who used his hands because they were strong, yet they were clean and soft.

He rolled away and gasped. "Oh, no. Look at the time! We'd better get dressed. Mom's got plans."

※

Frank and Celine joined his parents for breakfast.

His mother smiled. "I didn't want to wake the newlyweds. I know how it is when you're first married."

Celine blushed a brilliant red and he was certain he was, too. *If only they knew.*

His mom rambled on about her plans, and when they were done, he kissed Celine and went off with his dad. His father was considering a car and wanted Frank's opinion. Frank looked at the overpriced sports car sitting in the dealer's lot and agreed it was a real beauty. He knew his dad didn't really want his opinion about the car - he wanted his son's approval.

They did a few more things together and Frank

asked his dad to stop by the drug store long enough for him to grab a pack of gum. He skipped the gum, grabbed some mints, and a small package of condoms. He slipped the receipt and the items into his pocket. As he climbed into his dad's car, he offered his dad a mint.

When they returned to the house, it dawned on Frank that his father's world consisted of working, a few sports he enjoyed watching on the TV, an occasional round of golf with some friends, and virtually nothing else. Frank knew he never wanted his world to shrink like that. He wanted to go places and do things. He didn't want to watch it on TV, he wanted to be there and experience it. The first cycle accident had put the brakes on several things that he had wanted to do, but he wasn't going to let it stop him from enjoying everything else.

He stepped into his childhood home and looked around. Everything was perfect, right down to the folds in the draperies. It wasn't lived in; it was a museum. His mother's world was no different from his father's. Sadness cloaked him and turned into a sticky film. He wanted more out of life. Maybe he was no longer looking for the thrills, maybe he'd grown up, but he had come to the conclusion that he didn't want to aimlessly exist through life, he wanted to experience as much of it as he could.

After leaving a note on the foyer table asking to be awakened in time for dinner, he climbed the stairs. He needed a few hours of sleep. As he approached his bedroom doorway, he reached over his head and stretched. He could feel the difference in his right side, but he was certain in a few weeks any weakness would be a distant memory. Squinting his left eye, he looked through his right. He still couldn't see with it, but it was better than when he left the hospital. He opened his left eye and his door. There was Celine, sprawled across the bed, sleeping.

He would have laughed, but he was too tired to bother. Taking care not to disturb her, he lay next to her and closed his eyes. The next thing he knew, his phone was ringing.

"Dinner call," his mom giggled. "Be ready to leave in an hour."

"Thanks, Mom." He hauled himself from the bed and stretched.

He shaved while Celine dressed. Then she took over the bathroom and he changed into his brown wool suit. When Celine emerged from the bathroom, he couldn't remember her ever looking as pretty. She had a fancy braid in her hair that ended in a bun at the nape of her neck. Her pretty sweater top had a scalloped neckline, and she wore a charming double strand of old pearls with it. Elegant and understated, it was perfect for his family. "You look beautiful."

"Thank you."

"Did you run off with my mom?"

She shook her head. "I feigned a headache and took a nap. I know your one aunt wanted to meet me, but really I needed a few hours of sleep."

"I know. That nap did me a world of good. Okay, Mrs. Cresson, ready to face the rest of my family? So far you are doing great."

Celine pulled her scarf around her neck as Frank helped her into her coat.

Celine knew Brook Brooklyn, but meeting his father and mother was slightly different, especially since Brook and Nikki were not there. The house was large and very modern, completely opposite of Frank's childhood home. This house was also waterfront property and the view was spectacular. Every room appeared to be brimming with family, and children ran amuck.

Frank watched Celine. One by one, she charmed everyone and acted as though she were used to having servants with trays of hors d'oeuvres.

When Celine turned down the appletini and the hot hard cider, he asked her what she would drink.

"Good gin on a short tonic."

"No problem." He returned to her side a moment later with exactly what she wanted. He'd seen her serve every drink imaginable, but he'd never seen her drink. *This should be interesting.*

She appeared to get along well with his Aunt Michelle, and Celine did well with the cousins, including the ones he didn't like.

But deep inside, he was pleased that Brook and Nikki weren't in attendance. He knew they often went to visit Nikki's parents for Thanksgiving. He didn't want to have any discussion of him and Brook working together. What had happened between them was years ago, but obviously Brook had a long memory and wasn't about to forget. Besides, Frank had not decided what he wanted to do.

Ken Taylor's motorcycle business held more appeal than practicing law. Ken hadn't exactly asked, but Frank knew Ken wanted him. As it was, the most he could give Ken was a few hours each week. Ken needed someone everyday to run the company while he created motorcycles.

"You seem lost in thought." Celine smiled as she wrapped her arm around his waist.

"I was. Trying to make some decisions about my future. I want to talk to Ken Taylor." He steered

Celine onto the back porch. The air had a bit of nip to it, but it wasn't freezing.

Celine touched her forehead with the back of her hand. "How did you know I was roasting?"

Frank laughed. "For the same reason I was? It's hot in there. Are you having fun?"

She wrinkled her nose. "When I was little, we'd go to my grandmother's house and everyone was there! Tons of aunts and uncles, and lots of children, but I never remember misbehaving or any of my cousins being unruly. And it seemed as though the littlest ones were always passed from one set of arms to another." She motioned with her thumb. "It's crazy in there."

"Welcome to my family."

Celine raised her eyebrows. "I'm surprised you don't have armed guards at all the doors. There are more diamonds in there than in the jewelry store in Mariner's Cove."

"Hmm, maybe I should check them out, if they have diamonds as nice as what you'll find in this house."

Celine rolled her eyes. "Just how much money does your family have?"

"Honestly I'm not certain. I know that Brook's first wife decided to see if she could outspend what he made."

"Ouch."

"Oh, she did a number on him. She even slept with Arnie."

"Megan's husband?"

Frank nodded. "And now you know why Brook ran off to Mariner's Cove and prefers to avoid all the family get-togethers."

She shook her head. "I can't blame him."

"I can't believe Megan is staying with Arnie. I doubt she's still sleeping with him. She probably stays for the money."

Celine shuddered. "So much for the image of the perfect family. By the way, where might I find a bathroom room?"

"I'll show you. Everyone is probably using the one off the foyer or the one off the den." He steered her to a wing near the bedrooms. "His and her offices." He pointed to each side of the hall, checked a handle and the door opened easily. "Unoccupied. I'll be out there. So when you come out turn left, otherwise you'll wind up in their bedroom."

"That looks like another living room."

"It's their sitting room, and the bedroom is behind it. The other bedrooms are on the opposite wing."

"Oh. I promise I won't get lost."

He left her and joined his family. Charlotte was the cousin closest to him in age, and she had married the soccer player, Tito Renato. Unfortunately Frank's Spanish was about as bad as Tito's English, but they chatted about several games and some of the players.

The next thing he knew, everyone was being called to dinner. That's when he saw Celine again. Brook's mom had assigned seats, but a few people didn't like the arrangement, and then Bill wanted to sit on the end because he was left-handed. Frank leaned down and whispered in Celine's ear, "Musical chairs adult style."

Celine giggled and eventually Frank managed to take a place beside her.

Brook's father sat at the head of the table and called for everyone's attention. He had a short speech about being family, and he thanked everyone for coming. Then he formally introduced Celine as Frank's bride. Frank wanted to cringe as Celine's little lie had grown beyond an intimate handful of family members.

Dinner was served as though they were at a fine restaurant. About halfway through the meal, Megan put her fork down and demanded to know why Celine was wearing Aunt Susan's pearls.

Celine looked at Megan and then at Brook's mom.

"These are my pearls."

Megan turned to Brook's mom. "You promised them to me!"

Charlotte stood and came to where Celine was sitting. "They certainly look like yours, Aunt Susan. Gold clasp with five diamonds, double strand...besides, who wears pearls? They're so passé."

"I didn't give my pearls to anyone, and I'll prove it." Aunt Susan stood and walked out of the dining room.

Frank shook his head and put his hand on Celine's leg, hoping to assure her that this was just normal family infighting. He leaned over and whispered in her ear. "Don't listen to Charlotte. I think they look lovely on you."

A minute later, Aunt Susan returned. She stared at Frank. "I can't find my pearls."

Megan glared. "What else has she stolen while she's been here? Maybe we all need to check our purses!"

Chapter 5

*C*eline tried hard to keep her cool and her wits. She wasn't about to let anyone harass her, much less Frank's family. The allegation was unfounded. She could prove they were hers. She still had the letter that had accompanied them and the other things she inherited from her grandmother. But she wasn't about to stay and have Frank's family accuse her of theft.

She pushed her chair away from the table and slowly stood. "These are my pearls and I can prove it. I inherited them from my grandmother. But sitting here several hundred miles away from my house, I can't verify a darn thing. Furthermore, I don't appreciate anyone attacking my integrity." She looked at Frank. "I will not stay in a house and be treated this way. Your choice - are you coming with me or staying here?"

Frank stood. "Just a moment."

He grabbed at her wrist and she immediately shook her hand free, using a self-defense move Andy had taught her.

"I said just a moment!"

"I'm not staying another moment!" She began to walk away.

"And I can't blame her. Megan you had no right to say what you did. And, Aunt Susan, Celine is not a thief."

Celine heard his words from the hallway where she stood. She was pleased that he had stuck up for her, but still the pain from the family's attack was more than she could handle. Part of her wanted to cry and part of her wanted to scream. She had always lived her life above reproach. Mariner's Cove was a small town, the kind of place where if you did anything wrong, it seemed as though everyone knew about it. She had a reputation as a good kid, and as a trustworthy adult.

"Celine, I'm sorry. I don't know what got into Megan, and I'm really not sure what happened in there. But I'm positive you had those pearls around your neck before we left Mom and Dad's."

"Of course I did. And I can prove it. When we get back to the house, I'll sit in the car while you go upstairs and look in the room. You will find the blue box that they were in. Certainly I couldn't have rushed to your parents and planted the box there after I stole them from your Aunt Susan's bedroom."

"Good point. But before we leave, let's take some insurance with us."

"What do you mean?"

Frank took the car keys from Celine's hand. "And these are my insurance that you will stay right here."

He walked back inside and called to Brook's dad. "Uncle Archie, I know it's Thanksgiving, and I know with all the family here, this is the last thing you need. But I want you to come with me, or at least follow me to my parents, because I think we can settle this situation very quickly if you do. Celine did not steal Aunt Susan's pearls. The box that the pearls were in is still back at my parents'. There's no way she was at your house prior to today, and there's no way she could steal the pearls, put the box back at my parents, and return to your house without somebody realizing she was gone."

"Frank, this is serious. If she's stolen those pearls, my wife will press charges."

A knife twisted someplace in Frank's gut. "She didn't steal the pearls."

Uncle Archie grabbed up his keys and his coat. "I'll meet you in the driveway."

Frank walked back outside and handed Celine the keys as he slid into the passenger seat of the car. "You'd better not be lying."

There was something about the way Frank was acting that sent a cold chill through Celine's system. Having him doubt her was almost as bad as his family's accusations.

She was glad she had taken a nap, because she knew exactly what she needed to do. It would be a long night, and her heart was shattering into little fragments that tore at her soul.

The whole way back to Frank's parents' home, she assumed that it was Frank's parents following her. But when the car pulled next to her and Brook's father got out, she was more than a little surprised.

"Wait here. If that box from your pearls is in my bedroom, this whole situation is instantly settled. I don't want to even think what will happen if it's not."

Boiling hot blood rushed through her system. *Damn you, bastard!*

She didn't have long to wait for Brook's dad to reappear with the box in his hand.

"Celine, I'm really sorry. What was done to you was extremely unfair. Will you please come back to the house?" Uncle Archie appeared to be almost begging.

She opened her car door and climbed out. There was no going back - no undoing what had been done to her. No apology could negate the pain that they caused. Mustering all of her strength, she looked Uncle Archie in the eyes, held out her hand, and said, "I'll take my box."

He handed her the box. She took the blue box, walked inside, past Frank, and returned to the bedroom. It didn't take but a few minutes to pack her things. She knew other women, who would have allowed Frank's family's money to color their decision, but she believed that money was not an excuse for poor behavior.

Frank joined her. "What do you think you're doing?"

"I'm leaving. That's what I'm doing."

"Didn't Uncle Archie apologize and ask for you to return to his place?"

She chomped at her tongue. He might have showed support for her in front of his family, but his doubt in her is what broke her heart. She grabbed her suitcase, and he attempted to take it from her.

"No. I'm leaving, and I'm leaving here alone. It's over. I'll let you to figure out how to have a pretend divorce. I'm done. I'm going home."

"You can't just walk away."

"I can't? Watch me." She walked down the stairs and out the front door. Her entire body hummed with her anger as she climbed into the rented car. But she couldn't give into her fury.

Trying to find her way back to the interstate wasn't easy. After several wrong turns, she found a sign that pointed her in the right direction. She wound up on an unfamiliar road, but eventually she did find the interstate and she breathed a sigh of relief. She promised herself she'd stop someplace for coffee and a donut. *Certainly the truck stops are open.*

*

Frank stood there and watched her drive off. There was nothing he could do. He hadn't been released to drive, and with one eye not working, he didn't exactly trust himself. But he wasn't on city streets. He was in a private community. He grabbed his mom's keys and took her car back to Uncle Archie's.

When he arrived, everyone had finished eating and had retired to various rooms in the house. The talk was about Celine. Apparently his aunt's pearls had been found sitting in the safe.

He sat at the table with his uncle, and the caterer served them dinner. *What are the odds that they would own matching sets?*

His uncle held his fork poised above the slice of turkey breast. "Where's Celine?"

Frank swallowed. "She left. She's livid, and I really don't blame her."

The older man chewed his mouthful of food and swallowed it. "Why aren't you going after her?"

"I'm not cleared to drive. I'm on several medications that say I shouldn't be driving, and I can't see out of my right eye."

"But you drove here."

"Private community. With luck, I won't take out your neighbors' bushes on the way home."

Uncle Archie frowned. "You need to go after her."

Frank raised his shoulders and let them drop. "I've been thinking about how to do that. That might be the simplest part of a bigger problem."

"What do you mean?" Frank's father joined them at the table. "Certainly you two aren't having problems this early in your marriage."

Frank snorted. "This is going to sound totally crazy, but it's about time I debunk the little lie that we've been living." He paused and looked at both men. "We're not married."

"What?" His father's face held no expression. Lawyers work hard at not allowing any emotion to show on their face when hit with a surprise. And his father was the best.

"Explain!" Uncle Archie demanded.

Frank shook his head and ate another bite of food before he answered. "She told the hospital that we were newlyweds so she could see me. But when Mom showed up, Celine didn't dare let on otherwise. She assumed, and I believe correctly, that Mom would have told the hospital that we were not married to protect me. She had no idea who Celine was, and I certainly never said that I had married while I was in Mariner's Cove. But the lie circulated through this family faster than yellowjacket wasps at a picnic." He forked a portion of stuffing. "Truthfully, Celine and I barely know each other. The normal progression of dating was interrupted."

Frank's father put down his cup of coffee. "But on the recording of the accident, you call her your wife."

Frank shrugged and then grinned. "I don't remember a thing, so I'm going to assume that I had fallen in love with her, enough to be thinking of her in terms of marriage."

"And now what are you feeling?"

Frank glared at his dad. "After this fiasco? A whole lot of anger. But when it comes to Celine, I have a ton of respect for her. She handled herself with more dignity than most of the adult females that were in this room."

He held up one hand as he took his forkful of stuffing and ate it. "She works hard. She's not from a poor family - guess you'd call them middle class. But she has more class than most young women. Her manners are impeccable, and she's a strong independent woman who has never asked me for a penny. She's not after my money. If anything she's felt guilty over Mom buying her clothes. She's lived in Mariner's Cove her entire life, and although her parents have moved away, she's still very much a family-oriented person."

Uncle Archie broke into the conversation. "Those

pearls aren't paste."

Frank raised his eyebrows. "When her grandmother died, Celine, being the only female offspring, was gifted with quite a few things. As I said, I was never given the impression that the family was poor. I happened to think that she looked lovely." He finished the last of the food on his plate. "She would have looked just as lovely if those pearls had come from the dollar store."

A woman in uniform asked Frank if he'd like a cup of coffee and some pie.

He couldn't hold back his grin. "Yes, on the coffee, and a piece of both pumpkin and pecan, but skip the whipped cream. I should have left more room. That apple pie looks delicious especially warmed with cream on it."

"Frankie, I know you have space in your stomach." The woman laughed as she left the room.

Frank's father harrumphed. "Keep eating like that, and you'll have a heart attack before you are forty."

"Splurging a few times a year isn't going to hurt me."

"Probably not. But what are you going to do about Celine?"

✳

Celine called Crabby's and told them she was free to work.

Old Crabby's pleasure came through in his voice. "Our regular customers are asking for you."

Saturday night, she was back at Crabby's Pot House. The place was overflowing in customers. No matter how hard she tried to put the last five weeks behind her, she couldn't package the experience and mark it off. Somehow she kept waiting to see Frank's smiling face, but then the whole debacle with his family would flash in a single instant and remind her why she was home alone.

When she almost dropped an entire appetizer tray of seafood to the floor, Crabby yelled at her.

"Sorry! I'm off my game tonight."

"Well, stop acting like a love sick teen who just discovered that Davy Jones was married with a baby."

"Huh?"

"Never mind, he was before your time."

She raised her eyebrows and looked at the older man as she pushed through the swinging doors into the dining area.

But it was later that evening when she went into the bar for four drafts that she did a double take. She saw Brook Brooklyn and another man sitting together talking. The man's back was to her, yet she could have sworn it was Frank. She grabbed the drafts as soon as Andy poured them and returned to the dining room. But the knot in her stomach twisted tighter and tighter. She had to know to whom Brook was talking and, if it was Frank, why was he in town? *How did he get here?*

Every time she walked into the bar, she looked in Brook's direction, but not once could she catch a solid glimpse of the other man. She chastised herself. Had she not broken up with Frank? Had he not doubted her integrity? But she couldn't help herself. There was something about Frank that drew her to him like a magnet. The incident at his aunt and uncle's house played through her mind.

"Celine! The she crab soup!" the chef yelled.

She grabbed the bowl from the stainless steel counter and couldn't remember which table had ordered it. She flipped her order pad open. *Table 24.*

Out of the corner of her eye, she spotted Brook leaving. She headed for the kitchen and opened the big refrigerator. She grabbed up a White Cap. Similar to a parfait made with blueberries and blueberry ice cream, she placed it on a small tray and stopped at the bar long enough for Andy to add the liquor and top it off with whipped cream. She was determined to discover Brook's companion.

The man sat with his back to her as she sidled beside him. Now she knew it was Frank, and her mouth went dry. All those plans of what to say flew away. Instead, she mumbled, "This is on me."

Frank caught her wrist. "I talked to Brook."

"Yeah, I saw him with you."

"Can you sit for a moment?""

She shook her head.

"I want to talk to you."

"I'm busy."

"I'll wait."

The knot in her stomach grew ten times in size.

As the evening wound down, she rolled silverware in the dining room and did everything she could think of doing to avoid talking to Frank. But when the last call for alcohol went out, she knew she could no longer avoid him. She served the last round of drinks, handled the tabs, and then was faced with the inevitable - Frank.

She pulled out the stool across from him at the high top. "You wanted to talk? Make it quick I've got tons to do before I get out of here."

He slipped her his business card. "Let's pick this up from the beginning. I think we went into fast-forward without actually knowing each other. I only know what I feel when you are around, and what I feel when you aren't. Let's give this relationship the chance it deserves."

She picked up his card and pocketed it. "Sounds fair enough."

She started to stand, but he grabbed her arm.

He got that slight smile on his face. "One more thing before you go, well, two. You can call me, or you know where I live and where to get a great cup of coffee in the morning."

"I might enjoy a cup of coffee," she mumbled.

He took her hand into his and threaded their fingers. "I can't explain it, but knowing you were in the hospital with me... You did a lot and that means something to me. I don't think I knew it was you, but when you held my hand I could feel something very special. I still feel it."

Celine withdrew her hand and scurried away before tears welled in her eyes. She didn't want to feel anything. She wanted to hate him for not blindly trusting her. But the whole relationship had been tossed into a time warp that wasn't very realistic. She had learned a great deal about him, but he barely knew her. It would be wrong to judge him unfairly when so much felt so right.

She swiped at her eyes, being careful not to mess up her eyeliner and mascara. She needed to finish up for the night. *What am I going to do? Do I call him?*

＊

Frank returned to the yacht and looked around. She had put back everything she had taken to her place. His shirts and pants hung in the closet, but this time, they smelled like her. Not a perfumed scent, maybe... He couldn't place it. He breathed in and held it. An electrical current wrapped his hand - the one that had held hers.

He peeled off his clothes and took a shower. Warm water rolled over his body. His imagination took over and he pictured her there with him. He wanted to gather her into his arms and feel her naked body pressed to his. The desire to touch, feel, and penetrate her overwhelmed him. He closed his eyes and followed his thoughts.

When he slipped between the covers of his bed, he couldn't find solace. *Will she stop for coffee?*

Morning refused to come soon enough to suit him. He looked at the glowing numerals on the wall clock and saw 4:10, and then 5:19. When the timepiece said 6:36, he sprang from the bed, hit the shower long enough to wake up, and pulled on a pair of jeans and long-sleeved tee with a wool sweater over it. He straightened the bedroom, bathroom, and headed for the galley. He made a pot of coffee and then waited. With luck, he'd see Celine as she came through town.

At quarter to nine, he still had not seen her. He tried to tell himself that she was not avoiding him, but he wondered and worried. He poured another cup of coffee and kept his gaze peeled on the town's waterfront merchants. He could barely sit still. It dawned on him that he hadn't felt this way since he was racing. Each race sent an adrenalin rush into his system and tensed his muscles. He removed his arms off the armrests of his chair and shook them. It didn't help. He cursed under his breath.

Races went through his head. Skill was a huge factor, but the bike was everything. It had to take a pounding, yet be fast. He wasn't the right size to go pro, and he knew it. He was too tall and weighed too much. But that hadn't stopped him from enjoying the sport. He knew the professional riders, and there wasn't a thing he didn't know about the bikes. He'd eaten his fair share of dust, and knew how to pull into the top ten. But pulling in front was something he couldn't do. If he won, it was because the best made mistakes and went down.

Brook liked to sail. That was a gentlemen's sport, but racing cycles was too physical, too déclassé. Except he didn't care, he knew it was physical, but it also took brains. And he excelled at knowing what the bike needed for a particular course. The thrill of being part of a racing team was something he never got in a courtroom. That was always cut and dry. All he had to do in court was line up his ducks and go in blazing. He'd never lost a case.

He knew where his interest rested - squarely with motorcycles. Ken Taylor had been on Frank to join him. The concept of running the company appealed to him and that would free Ken so he could design and build. Frank knew he had what it took to lead; yet he'd still be active in the whole cycle process. This was the less physical end, and almost required a background in law. It was the perfect job.

He didn't want to be part of Brook's office, nor did he want to go back to his father's. Living here meant he was a few hours away from Ken, but it wasn't that far. *A home office...?*

He almost missed seeing Celine. He raised his

arms and hollered at her. She held up one finger and walked to the bank's little night drop. Then she scampered in his direction. He met her on the dock and escorted her to the yacht.

"I was concerned that you wouldn't come." Frank helped her onto the yacht.

She raised her shoulders and let them drop. "I spent half the night trying to decide if I wanted to see you again."

"But you are here."

"Don't get your hopes up. Nothing is simple." She took the cup of coffee Frank offered her. "Thanks. Maybe our relationship was doomed from the start."

"How can you say that?"

"Simple. Look at what has happened."

"I know, and for the record, my dad and Uncle Archie know that the whole newlywed thing is a farce. I told them."

"How'd they handle it?"

He rolled his palms up. "In a way, I think my dad was relieved. He was concerned that I'd done some totally irrational thing. Then he must have told my mom, as she fired so many questions at me."

"Wonderful." She grimaced.

"I think she was disappointed. She likes you."

"That's nice to know." She sipped at her coffee.

"I'm just not sure how to start over."

"Well, today is Sunday, and I think we were going to visit an apple orchard when everything went haywire. The problem is I can't drive. Any possibility of visiting that orchard?"

Celine smiled at him. "If you don't mind riding in my car, I think it can be arranged. I'm sure they still have apples and plenty of cider." She cocked her head. "Do you remember our plans for that day?"

"Not a speck of memory. But you have since told me what our plans had been prior to the accident." He looked at her and grinned. "But it does feel like the movie, *Groundhog Day*. I'm going to cross my fingers that this Sunday goes better than that one."

✻

An hour later, Celine was headed northwest as she took Frank in her car to Clifford's Orchard. They drove though the countryside with patchwork fields in shades of pale gold and beige, and then through forests that had dropped their leaves, leaving dark barren arms to stretch towards the sky while russet foliage carpeted the ground.

He told her that he'd made some decisions. He

wasn't going to return to the law practice. Instead, he intended to call Ken Taylor in the morning and step into the position of running Tayson. "It's where I want to be. I still want that thrill of competition without being the rider. I like the idea of creation and of being in the forefront of a new company."

"And your parents?"

"They are going to be disappointed. I told Brook last night that I had no designs on trying to partner with him, and I intended to go to Tayson. I also apologized profusely for being such a stupid ass when I spent that summer with him."

"I hope he's forgiven you, after all, you were still a kid."

"I wasn't that much of a kid, and I was *extremely* selfish and irresponsible. But I believe he's forgiven me."

Celine made several right turns and the last one put her on a narrow road filled with hairpin curves that went up the side of mountain. At the top was the orchard. The parking lot was almost deserted, but the cider barn was open. They bought two one-gallon jugs of cider and a jug of hard cider. They each indulged in a candy apple and several other things, including dehydrated apple chips. They put everything in the trunk of her car except for their candy apples, which they took to a bench. Sitting there, munching, they had a grand view of the valley below.

The joy that flowed through him as they sat was indescribable. The simple pleasure of being in the country with a view that stretched for miles combined with the crispy cool air that was totally odorless would have been enough to satisfy him, but having Celine at his side made everything perfect.

Celine attempted to wipe her red, candy-coated chin. He wound up laughing at her as she attempted to remove the sticky, red stain.

She quit trying to use a napkin and began to rub her chin with an exposed bit of apple. She managed to make the red mark appear to be a pale pink.

He cupped her chin in his hand and turned her face to him. "Have I told you how beautiful you look to me?"

"I don't think you've said that today."

"Then let me say it. You are an amazingly beautiful woman, even with a pink chin, which now matches your pink cheeks."

"Thank you," she mumbled as her eyes closed and her lips parted.

It was an offer to kiss her that he wasn't about to turn down. His lips touched hers and fireworks went off in his lower abdomen. She wrapped her arms around him and clung to him as though she were in danger of falling from a cliff.

Oh, yeah.

The sound of someone walking nearby broke their lips apart. But the feeling inside of him lingered. He wanted her.

She blinked her brown eyes at him and his cheeks pulled the edges of his mouth upwards. She was everything he wanted in a female. But how could he make her understand? Had he not been the skeptical one? Why had he even considered what Megan said? He knew she liked to create problems. He could have waited. No. He should have waited. Now he was kicking himself. Was it even possible to build a relationship when the foundation had been cracked?

Chapter 6

When Celine said goodnight to Frank, the feeling was similar to a wave washing over the bulkhead and onto the street. She couldn't stop the exciting force of love, yet somehow that wave seemed to drain away too quickly, leaving her feeling cold and alone.

That night she stared into the darkness and tried to figure out exactly what had gone wrong. That horrible Thanksgiving meal played again and again in her mind. *Had he really doubted me? Or was I so stressed I that went into a defense mode?*

When morning came, she was back to her routine. With her feet in fuzzy slippers, and wearing an old set of sweats to keep her warm, she sat at her computer and pulled up the first lab client. It took her only a few seconds to complete the billing. The second one wasn't as a simple, but still didn't take her very long. The blood test code was there for the insurance company, so it was more a matter of checking everything before pressing the send button. Many weren't quite as simple, but most were. Speed and accuracy is what counted, and she'd been doing the billing for so long she had both.

When her doorbell rang, she was so deep into what she was doing that she almost didn't hear the chimes playing behind her. She went to her door and discovered Frank on the other side.

"Hi. What brings you here so early?"

"You didn't come to the yacht for coffee."

She rolled her eyes. "It's Monday. I have to work, remember?"

"Oh." The disappointment showed in his eyes.

"If you are quiet, you may drink my coffee and watch me."

He shrugged and followed her into the kitchen. She went back to her billing and left him to fend for himself. After he drank two cups of coffee, he wordlessly kissed her check and left. She had a job and she had no intention of giving it up to entertain him.

Friday morning, she met him and they had brunch

together, and then they went to look at the house. Saturday was her day for grocery shopping and other such things so he came with her. And Sunday was their day together, which included a nice dinner. But the third Saturday in December, Frank had asked her to take off from working at Crabby's. It was Brook's big Christmas party at the Groton Hotel, and most of the merchants in Mariner's Cove, along with many of the local residents, would be in attendance, including Crabby.

"What am I supposed to wear to this big party?"

"A little black Versace dress with plenty of bling."

"I don't own either one. I don't even own a plain black dress."

Frank blew out a breath. "Okay, what's something like that cost?"

"How should I know? Forty dollars?"

"You're joking, right?" Frank opened his wallet and counted out several bills. "Here's nine hundred. If you need more, let me know."

"You are crazy!"

"More?"

"No! I don't even know where I'd buy a dress for two hundred dollars, much less nine."

"Just buy a dress. Something pretty."

"There's that pretty red sweater on the mannequin

in the dress shop. I could get that with a pair of black slacks."

He shook his head. "I want you in a cocktail dress. You can bet Ivy will be in a tuxedo and Nikki will be wearing something very formal."

"Who is Ivy?"

"Brook."

"I'm sorry, I forgot."

Frank nodded.

"Okay, one little fancy dress. But I hate black. It looks horrible on me."

"Get what you want."

Tuesday afternoon she finished working for the medical laboratory company and headed to Mason's, the tiny dress shop facing the harbor. She wanted that red sweater. It wasn't screaming red, but it was red and would look great on her. They still had her size and she bought it. Then she looked at dresses. After trying on several, she gave up.

"CeCe, I want you to try this one." The shop owner came out of the back and handed her a rather odd sparkly gold dress that hung on the hanger like a limp rag. "I swear this looks much better on."

Celine rolled her eyes as she took the ugly thing to the dressing room. She slipped it on before deciding she must have put it on backwards and turned it around.

The dress fell to slightly below her knees, the back draped open almost to her waist, and every curve on her body was accented. The owner was right. The dress didn't look the same on her as it did on the hanger. She slid her hands down her hips and then over her backside. *Maybe I'm too fat to wear this.*

"CeCe, that looks as though it was made for you." The shop owner stuck her nose into the dressing room area. "Perfect, perfect, perfect! You'll need a really nice pair of heels. Something that comes to your ankle."

Celine nodded at the older woman. "I don't know. I'm not a person to wear sparkles, and he did say black dress for the Christmas party."

"Darling, anyone can do a black dress, but you'll be the belle of the ball in this."

Celine pressed her lips together and turned around once more to see herself in the mirror. "What do I wear for jewelry?"

The woman showed her several things, but Celine turned her nose up at all of them. She didn't have time to kill. She had to get to Crabby's.

Wednesday morning, she took Frank to the doctor's office and she went shopping at the nearby mall. She found the perfect pair of shoes and some

Christmas jewelry to wear with her new dress. When her phone buzzed, she knew it was Frank.

Frank greeted her with a big smile. "I'm cleared to drive."

"Fantastic!"

"I know you are delayed, so why don't you drop me at the car rental place and head on home. I don't want to keep you away from your job any longer."

She nodded, but she didn't think her mood could be any better. "What did the doctor say about your eye?"

"She said those nerves are healing at a faster rate than she expected, and I'll just have to be very careful while driving to compensate for it, but she thought I'm doing great. No seizures or anything - not even wicked headaches. It's all good news."

Celine had one more question and wasn't certain she wanted to hear the answer. "What about Ken Taylor?"

"I talked to Ken last night. Unfortunately, it's virtually impossible to talk to you when you're at Crabby's." He reached over and put his hand on her leg. "I officially start January 2. I'll probably need to spend a week or two there. It's important that I catch up on everything that is happening, and I know what Ken has in the works. But after that, I'll only go there occasionally. Ken and I need to work out where we want the physical home office to be, but for now, most of it will be done by computer and phone from wherever I happen to be."

She nodded. "Sounds good."

"No enthusiasm in your answer."

She shrugged. "I was hoping you'd stay in Mariner's Cove, since you are redoing the house."

"Oh, I'm staying. But I will be facing some traveling. Plus it's fun to watch the races."

"But you won't be riding."

"Not competitively, but I'll always ride. What happened was a fluke. If I had been in a car, my injuries would have been different, but the hit I took on that cycle would have probably sent a car spinning and possibly killed someone. We all survived, including the kid who caused the accident."

"I heard he was high." She took the exit off the main road.

"All three of them in that car were high. Drugs are bad. I know I sound like a parent, but as a lawyer, I've handled too many cases involving drugs. Even when they don't think they are high, they are high. There's a reason why there are warnings on over-the-counter drugs, such as cold medications."

"You don't have to lecture me. I don't want to take

anything. The last time I took anything, I was twelve, and I had a strep throat. If I get a headache, it's usually because I haven't had enough sleep. A nap is a great cure-all for me."

"Even a cold?"

"I'll repeat. The last time I was sick, I was twelve. It's rare for me to catch anything."

"You're lucky."

She pulled into the car rental. "See you at Crabby's?"

After she dropped Frank off, she went home and changed into her uniform. With a peanut butter sandwich beside her, she worked at her computer, doing billing, until she had to stop and still was a few minutes late getting to Crabby's.

It seemed that lately Crabby couldn't keep a wait staff, and she had no idea why. Crabby was constantly asking her to wait tables on her days off. But the tourist crowd was dwindling and she knew she wouldn't be very busy. As usual, it was only Lisa and Andy working. Lisa would help cover any overflow and bus the tables, leaving Celine to wait tables.

Frank showed up early and left when she did. He walked her home, which was nice. Mariner's Cove had always been a safe place to live, but having Frank with her made her feel safe and protected. And his goodnight kiss warmed every part of her body. Starting over was a good thing, but in a way, she hated it. It would have been nicer if he lived with her and even better if he shared her bed.

"Come to the yacht tomorrow for a quick cup of coffee. I have two surprises for you."

"I have to work."

"I know you do, that's why I said a quick cup of coffee."

And I have a surprise for you. If only I can find the time to pull it off!

✳

Frank decided that the nice thing about living on the yacht was waking early. The sounds of the watermen getting ready for their day was better than any alarm clock. But today the yacht rocked against its ropes. White caps even appeared in the cove and the wind off the Atlantic made it seem twice as cold. He poured his coffee in a travel mug to keep it hot while he waited for Celine, and he crossed his fingers that she would come.

She came wearing flannel-lined jeans and a heavy parka. He greeted her with a cup and showed her the car that he rented, but he also showed her his cycle sitting next to it.

"Factory restored! And good as new."

"Um, isn't it a little cold to be riding?"

He grinned. "Follow me, my beautiful woman."

On board, he handed her a package. She opened it and got a very confused look on her face. "What is it?"

"Your winter riding suit. It's heated. Temperature controlled." He showed her the pigtail that plugged into the motorcycle.

"Thank you. You are incorrigible."

"I know, and it drives my family nuts. Which...speaking of family, I do hope you intend to have Christmas here in Mariner's Cove, because I have plans for that day, too. But I was hoping I could sneak you off to your parents for a few days. I thought maybe we could drive down and visit them."

"Not on the motorcycle!"

"I figured we'd take the car - that's why I rented it. A woman wants to bring a dozen suitcases with her. Especially over a holiday."

"I'm not that bad."

"Then it's a deal?"

She rocked her hand. "Crabby isn't going to be thrilled, and getting off from the lab might be a problem. They slow down, but they expect us to continue to work at least half time."

"Well don't say anything until Monday to either one. I still have a few hurdles to overcome so that I'm completely free to take off."

She raised her eyebrows.

He couldn't hold back the chuckles. *If you only knew what was in store for you!*

He smiled as he informed her that he would go to the house Friday morning by himself. "I feel guilty keeping you from your job this week."

"Going by yourself is probably a good thing. I have *so* much to do!" She finished her cup of coffee, thanked him, and left for her home.

That morning, he went to Mariner's Cove's little jewelry store. It catered mostly to tourists, but kept a generous supply of things like engagement rings for locals and tourists alike. Except he had no clue as to her size, and it hadn't even crossed his mind. The store refused to help him until he could tell them a size.

Frustrated, he left and wandered through the town. Then it dawned on him that if he could get his hands on the set that she wore when she claimed she was his wife...

He stopped at the grocery store for some nice luncheon meats and rolls, and then went to the local coffee shop for a pound of their finest coffee. Bearing gifts of food would get him in the door, and then he'd have to figure out a way to get his hands on those rings.

His plan worked. He fixed lunch and then said he was going to borrow her keys.

"Why?" She never even looked up from her computer screen.

"That way you don't have to get up every time I knock on your door."

"You know where I keep them."

They were sitting in a bowl on her bureau along with several other things, including that ring set. He scooped up the rings and the keys.

"See you soon!"

"You'd better be here before I have to leave for work, or I can't lock up behind me."

"I'll be back here in an hour."

He stopped at the hardware store and had a key made, and then went to the jewelry store. "These are a hair's breadth too large on her finger. They slide around."

The jeweler took them and measured them. "They are a five. We can go under by half a size, and that should tighten things up. If it's too tight, I can stretch them, or if they are still too loose, I can add a little to them."

"That will work." He had a feeling she would protest against a large showy ring, especially while working for Crabby, but he didn't intend for her to continue to work. She didn't need to work. "Show me your best."

He picked out a ring that swirled one way and then seemed to curl back onto itself. It was feminine, different, slightly old-fashioned looking, and he decided it would be perfect on her.

Frank hurried back to Celine's apartment. He let himself in and Celine was busy typing. He put her keys and her rings back, fixed a fresh pot of coffee, and tried to act as though he'd spent the day doing nothing.

He hoped that his plans meshed with hers, because he wanted her more than anything else.

Celine woke to her alarm ringing. It was all she could do to pull herself from the warmth and comfort of her bed. She only wanted to stay cocooned under her blankets. But once she had her shower, she was ready to face her day, and she had plans!

The first thing she did was go to the attic and drag down boxes of Christmas decorations. The first year she was alone, she put up a tree, but then decided it wasn't worth it and hadn't bothered since then. Now she had a reason to celebrate Christmas. Or did she? *He's getting a tree!*

She fixed a quick breakfast and then began to sort through the boxes. She found four strings of colored lights that worked and then picked through the ornaments that had hung on the family tree. Everything needed to be weatherproofed and she wondered about a few things. She put the decorations she was taking with her into a plastic bin and loaded it into the trunk of her car. Now she needed a tree. She drove over to the waterfront and checked for Frank's car. It was gone. *Good!*

She swung by the local high school for a tree from the student council society. "I want a tree that's not too tall and it has to be skinny."

"Really?"

She smiled at the young boy who didn't look old enough to even be in high school, but she knew he had to be. For years, she had worked their Christmas tree lot, as it was their biggest moneymaker of the year.

The young man led her to a tree in the center of

their lot. "Here it is. No one wants it."

"Well, it just found the perfect home for the holiday."

It wasn't just skinny - it looked almost flat on the one side. That just meant it would fit perfectly in the one corner.

"Do you want it bagged ma'am?"

She nodded. It wasn't that many years ago that she graduated from Mariner's Cove's High School. She had been an honors student, but she had no desire at the time to go to college, and she still didn't.

She stuffed the tree into her car and the top of it poked out her passenger window. At least she didn't have far to go.

Fortunately, Frank was still gone when she went to his yacht. She hefted the tree onto her shoulder and took it aboard. Then she returned to her car for the ornaments.

It took her longer than she expected to get it into the tree stand. The bag became the tree's skirt. Somehow she managed to get it decorated and get out of there before Frank returned.

She had one more thing on her list, a chimenea. Frank could use it on the yacht or on his patio once he moved. When the salesman explained the differences between the various ones in stock, she bought the more expensive one.

When she returned to her house, she ran the vacuum, did a little laundry, and got ready for work. She looked at her new dress hanging in her closet and smiled. Fairly certain that Frank would be pleased she crossed her fingers. The only thing that still worried her was Frank's announcement of his new job. She'd grown accustomed to seeing him daily and being with him. She hated the idea that he'd be gone.

She thought about that as she walked to work. It wasn't that he'd be gone - it was the fear that he would find someone else and leave her. *I want you, Frank. I've fallen in love with you.*

Frank was there at Crabby's door waiting for her.

"Hi. I know you are behind that Christmas tree, so don't try to deny it."

She grinned at him. "I hope you like it."

He followed her inside the restaurant. "It's the best tree I've ever seen, and you know why? Because it came from you and you've given me bits and pieces of yourself. I love it."

She threw her arms around him and kissed him. "I'm so happy that you love it."

"I love you, Celine. With all my heart, I love you."

Crabby fussed, "Are you going to work or stand there sucking face all night?"

Celine lifted her shoulders and let them drop. "I'm trying to take care of your best customer, after all, he hasn't missed a night here in weeks."

Andy laughed. "CeCe, that man is worth kissing."

As Frank sat at a high top table near the bar, he looked at Andy.

Celine fell into giggles. "He's mine, Andy." She turned from Andy to Frank. "Don't worry, he's knows you belong to me."

"Ah, CeCe, you take the fun out of everything." Andy hung the glass he had polished. "There's nothing like watching a hetero man squirm."

"You wouldn't do that to him, anyway. You have a partner."

Andy raised his eyebrows and laughed. "You're right, it's more fun toying with the women."

Crabby let Lisa go home early and then they got busy. When Celine got off, she was exhausted. Friday nights were always long, but the big tips weren't there, which just made it a long night.

Frank didn't walk her to her place - he walked her to his. She could feel the panic building inside, and with it came an excitement, but she was exhausted. She wanted to tell him she was too tired, and that he'd chosen the wrong night to be amorous. Her body tensed. *If I say it, he'll think I'm turning him down.*

He sent her into his bathroom to shower and handed her his robe to wear. She managed to wash the night's scent of food and drinks from her body and replaced them with the masculine scents of pine and patchouli. His robe fell to her ankles and would have wrapped her twice if it hadn't had sleeves.

She stepped out of the bathroom and Frank stood there waiting with a glass of wine. "Here. It's my turn. I'll only be a few minutes. Make yourself at home."

She looked around. He had lit candles and turned down the bed. It was so like him to try hard to be romantic. She appreciated what he'd done, but she could barely keep her eyes open. As she took a sip of her wine, she sat on the edge of his bed. Then put her glass down and curled into the big soft bed. It seemed that she heard her name being called, but she was too tired to chase the distant voice.

She opened her eyes to sunlight and Frank sitting beside her.

"How are you feeling, sleepyhead?"

She pointed her toes and raised her arms above her head. "What time is it?"

"It's time for breakfast."

She giggled. "Did we have fun last night?"

"I thought I'd thought of everything – obviously not. I hope you slept well."

She stretched one more time. "Tonight is your cousin's party."

"I can't wait. How about you?"

"Since when did guys get excited about a party? Most I know dread getting dressed up and behaving as though their mother taught them manners."

He laughed at her. "Hey, I'm not that bad! And I have a surprise for you, but not until tonight."

He leaned over and kissed her, every part of her responded to his moves. Covers vanished, and her heart strummed. Her skin begged for his kisses, and each kiss sent heat surging through her entire being. He was everything she had ever imagined.

Every move was soft and sexy. The pace was urgent but unhurried. He rolled her on top and let her take the lead. She heard herself cry out with delight.

Two bodies, meshed as one, working in unison like some well-orchestrated dance. His every action stoked her desire, yet told her how much she was appreciated. He slipped her under him. It was as though he worshiped her with every kiss and caress. Never had she been so wrapped in love or wanted so much to return the adoration so that he could experience it, too.

Their pace quickened, as they seemed to ascend to

a sexual peak. Higher and higher, they climbed, each urging the other onward until they had reached the point where their spirits became one.

When it ended, they continued to kiss and touch as though the thought of ending the encounter was beyond comprehension. Then suddenly the wind had left the sails and they both stilled. He rolled onto his back but brought her with him so that she was curled to his side. His breath fluttered through her hair.

His voice was hoarse as he whispered, "That was the most incredible thing I've ever experienced."

She hummed her response, still not ready to talk. Her hand found his and she threaded her fingers with his. It was something that they had done hundreds of time, yet that tiny act held so much meaning. Whatever just happened, she didn't want it to ever end. Then she wondered why she had waited so long.

Oh, please don't let this end.

✻

Frank couldn't believe how phenomenal the morning had been. What he had missed by her falling asleep was returned tenfold. How many times had he lain awake fighting his urges to have sex with her? Except he didn't just have sex, he'd made love to her, and not once but multiple times.

He opened the drawer where he had placed the ring he had bought for her. Lifting the lid on the box, he looked at the ring. His mind swirled with thoughts.

Maybe he should have gone to New York and bought her something specifically designed for her, but she wouldn't have cared. She wasn't like that. She would be thrilled even with a tiny diamond, because he knew it wasn't the money, it was the thought behind it. He closed the box and took a shower.

Two hours later, he checked his image in the mirror. Black wasn't his best color, but he'd softened the black tuxedo with a pale green shirt and a dark green bow tie and vest. He bared his teeth to the reflection, making certain his pearly whites were as white and as perfect as he could get them.

Mentally crossing his fingers, he headed to his rental car. His nerves were shot. He felt as though his body crawled with millions of tiny insects. Twice he shoved his hand into his pocket to make certain her ring was still there. *What if...? I'm not going to think about that!*

Chapter 7

Frank fumbled in his pocket for the key to Celine's apartment and then decided he'd knock. If it hadn't been so cold, he was certain his body would have been covered in perspiration. He wanted this evening to be perfect.

Celine greeted him in a gold dress that seemed to sparkle with her every move. Her russet-colored ponytail was now in a figure eight at the nape of her neck. To say she was exquisite was an understatement. Her shoes were dark green and made her look several inches taller. Her dark green jewelry was probably plastic, but she wore it like it was made from the finest jade. And her smile sent an instant pulse of heat through his system.

"By any chance did you pack an overnight bag? I'm

hoping I don't have to bring you home tonight."

She giggled. "Give me a few minutes and I'll have something ready."

He followed her into her bedroom.

"What do you want me bring?"

"Skip the pajamas. You look wonderful naked."

She raised her eyebrows. "And what about tomorrow? Do you have plans?"

"Nothing set in stone."

She grinned and vanished into her bathroom. A moment later she appeared with several things in her hands. She dropped them on her bed and then pulled a bag from her closet. Black jeans and a sweater were placed in her bag along with the stuff from her bed. It didn't take her three hours to decide what to wear. There was no fretting. She simply chose a few things and packed them. He grabbed the duffle and placed it by her front door while he helped her into her plain black coat.

"You look fantastic."

"Thank you."

Brook had asked Frank to come slightly early. He and Celine arrived about an hour before everyone else in Mariner's Cove. Brook was there looking like death warmed over in his tuxedo and Nikki looked glamorous in her black velvet cocktail dress. Maybe

Nikki and Celine had more in common than Frank had ever realized.

Celine jumped in and helped Nikki with the placement of nametags at the tables, and Celine immediately switched one couple for another. "Bad blood, and I have no idea why."

Nikki nodded. "Anyone else?"

Celine took the list from Nikki. "Not that I see."

"Thanks, CeCe. I'll remember that. I think we've got most of the town coming tonight. The first year we did this, barely anyone came. Now everyone comes."

"I'm surprised you've mixed the merchants with the watermen."

"Why?"

"Some people don't consider them businessmen."

"Oh, but they are."

"Well, yeah, I know that." Celine put the last set of tags on a table. "They have a boat or boats instead of a store or office. They work hard for their money." She giggled. "They also play hard."

Someone from Groton Hotel came and adjusted the lighting in the ceiling and then along the walls before beginning to light the candles on all the tables.

Brook came into the room with Frank. Brook motioned for them to come. "It's almost five o'clock.

Can't wait to see this."

"What?" Celine took Frank's hand as they stepped out a side door and onto a stretch of lawn that faced the Atlantic Ocean. A moment later, she gasped as a bright light filled the sky. "I realized they were working on it."

Brook smiled. "It cost a fortune to restore, but this town needed it. The Coast Guard gave us permission. And thanks to Frank helping with the cost, we managed to make it happen."

"It's beautiful." Nikki watched the light coming from the newly restored lighthouse that was part of the Groton Hotel. "We were so lucky that the Fresnel lens was still intact."

Brook put his arm around his wife's waist. "The mayor wanted a big lighting ceremony, but I decided this was a better way to celebrate."

"I think it's wonderful, and I'm so proud of both of you." Celine rubbed her arms. "But I'm freezing out here."

The dinner was lovely, and before the dancing started, the mayor and several people from the town council presented Brook and Frank with a plaque, acknowledging them as donors for the restoration. The small brass sign would be placed in the hotel lobby.

Celine knew the cousins had money. She saw that in the family Thanksgiving dinner. But when she heard the amount of money that had been spent for the restoration, the air went into her lungs and stayed there. She couldn't imagine anyone tossing that sort of money around as though it was nothing. She forced herself to breathe out slowly.

Brook thanked everyone for coming. "Now, let's get this party started!"

The band began to play a lively country song as Frank and Brook returned to the table. Frank grinned at Celine, and she couldn't help but smile back. He was a different build from Brook. Bigger and more solid than his cousin, yet, when she first saw Frank, there was something familiar about him, then she found out he was related to Brook.

"May I have this dance?" Frank extended his hand.

*

Celine stood and walked with Frank to the dance floor. Brook and Nikki followed. Soon several other guests had joined them. After several dances, they went back to their seats. He ordered drinks for the both of them. Maybe he needed some liquid courage.

He fingered the ring in his pocket. He also didn't want Celine putting too much thought in her answer. He only wanted a simple yes from her.

He watched her sipping at her drink. He knew she'd sip one drink for the entire night. She wasn't much of a drinker, and he knew those who don't drink feel it faster than those who do. He didn't want her drunk.

The ring in his pocket was burning holes in his very fiber and zapping his courage. He didn't want it to do either one. "I'll be right back."

He went to the band and spoke to the main guy. As a song came to an end, Frank grabbed the microphone. The band began to play, *You Light Up My Life*. Celine was the light of his life and *he was certain* that he'd surprise her by singing that old love song.

He released the microphone from the stand and walked to where she was sitting as he sang the last few lines. Then the band wound down the song, and he pulled the ring from his pocket. "Marry me."

His heart fell into his stomach as tears rolled down Celine's cheeks. He held the microphone behind his back and prayed she'd say yes. He whispered, "I love you. Please say yes."

More tears streamed down her cheeks.

Brook took the microphone from Frank and Nikki nudged Celine. "Say yes, Celine."

The band started to play another song but most eyes were on Frank and Celine. The stares from the other guests were boring into Frank like two hundred laser beams. Frank finally stood and grinned at the guests. "I think I shocked and overwhelmed her."

Nikki rolled her eyes at Frank. "Take her outside. Give her a few minutes without everyone watching her. There's not a face in this crowd that she doesn't know. CeCe, will you go with him?"

Celine nodded her response and Brook placed a white hankie in her hand.

Frank took her out to the porch that overlooked the cove. The cold air almost took his breath away after being in the warm room. Or was the room warm because he was nervous? He wasn't certain, but he also knew that it was probably too cold for her in that gold dress. Slipping his tux jacket off, he put it around her shoulders. He wasn't going to freeze to death, but he didn't want her catching a cold. Not that he ever believed someone would catch a cold from being cold, but maybe it was different for women. He didn't know.

Celine wiped at her tears. "You really want to marry me - for real?"

"Yes, for real. I don't want to wait until June to do it." He slipped the ring on her finger. "If you want something bigger, I'll get it for you."

She swiped at more tears that kept rolling down her face.

"Please don't cry. I'm not good with women who cry. It makes me feel like a total jerk, because I can never figure out how I'm supposed to respond. If you have a problem, just tell me. But don't cry."

"I've never been happier in my life than I've been with you. And this morning was beyond words." She mumbled as she wiped away tears and blew her nose.

"Then just say yes. A simple yes. That's all I need. We can plan the wedding later. Come on, I'm trying very hard to be romantic. I picked out that song because it sums up my feelings for you. And I was thinking that the light from the lighthouse would somehow be that symbol of our love and commitment. You'll know from this evening forward you light up my life. Okay, that's lame, I know."

"I really want to be married to you."

"Then say yes. What's so difficult with saying yes?"

"Because I'm saying yes to more than just a guy with a motorcycle." She blew her nose one more time. "Let me try to explain it." She sniffled. "Little girls all dream of fairies spinning beautiful ball gowns out of spider webs and then those fairies will sneak them out of the house so they can dance with Prince Charming who will instantly fall in love with them and ask them to marry him. Except we grow up and realize how stupid it is. We're lucky if we meet a guy who honestly cares about us, and with luck, makes enough money to take their family of two point three children to someplace like Disney World at least once before the kids are too old to care."

"I can take you there if that's what you want."

She rubbed her forehead with her fingertips. "That's just it. The entire time I've known you, you haven't worked, yet you can afford to pay half the restoration of the lighthouse and buy a home that was outrageously priced and then practically demolish it and start over. That's crazy unreal. And now you are going to go be the president of some little motorcycle company that you've funded from the get-go?"

"So where's the problem?"

"Don't you see? It's not real."

"No, it is real. No matter what I do or don't do, I have a trust fund. It's not unlimited, and believe me, I pushed those limits this year. If it weren't for Brook pushing the family over the lighthouse, we wouldn't have gotten that money. It is our gift to the town because we live here." He threaded his fingers with hers. "You've grown up here, and we were summer kids. You know darn well that newcomers, especially those with money, aren't exactly accepted. It was our way of buying acceptance. It's why that room is packed. The first time Brook had a Christmas party, he couldn't get but a few people to come. Now almost every merchant is here, along with the watermen."

"Okay, but kids like me who grow up in an average family don't get asked by Prince Charming."

"For starters, I'm not Prince Charming. I'm the wayward son who loves motorcycles more than a courtroom. I've bucked everything my parents ever wanted for me. But now I see a chance to do something I want to do. I know I'm starting almost from scratch, but I'm positive that Ken and I can build our own empire. We know the industry, know the competitive circuit, and we know what makes a motorcycle great."

He brought her fingers to his lips and kissed them. "You stuck by me when you didn't even know if I would survive."

She nodded. "I felt so guilty. You were coming to pick me up. And you'd been so nice to me."

"I think I fell in love with you from the moment I laid eyes on you."

She nodded. "I felt the same way. I knew you were special. And I'm freezing."

"So am I. But you haven't said yes or no."

"Why don't you get our coats and let me go home. I know my makeup is smeared down my cheeks."

"Okay, I'll take you home."

He vanished inside long enough to grab their coats.

But Brook stopped him. "Did she give you an answer?"

"Not yet."

Brook shook his head. "You're still crazy."

"I know."

Frank helped Celine into her coat and then drove to her apartment. In the light of her little living room, he could see the dark streaks from her makeup. He gave her time to redo her face. But after a few minutes, worry crept up his spine and landed squarely on his shoulders with a death grip.

He stood and went to her bathroom and tapped on the door before he opened it.

It looked as though she was combing her eyelashes.

"I'm glad I'm not a female."

"So am I."

"I meant that eye thing."

"I know what you meant." She picked up the vial of mascara and used that brush on her eyelashes. "I assume that you want me perfect."

"You are perfect. You're perfect for me." He leaned down and kissed the nape of her neck. "I don't want a female who will demand a couple hundred thousand dollar necklace that she probably won't wear more than twice. I want a woman who will enjoy a ride in the country and a candy apple. I want a woman who puts her heart into a Christmas tree and doesn't have to call in an interior decorator to do it." He chuckled. "That's the first Christmas tree I've ever had in my life."

"What?"

"Little Jewish boys don't grow up with Christmas trees. I was always a little envious of my gentile friends."

"Oh, my gosh! I had no idea. Now I feel like a complete idiot."

"Why? Because I don't walk around wearing a yarmulke?"

"What's that?"

"I can see we're going to have lots to learn. Marry me and we'll have a lifetime to learn together."

She scrunched up her face. "So, where did you learn to sing like that?"

"I don't know. I always enjoyed singing. My dad caught me singing a couple of pop tunes when I was about fourteen, and he shuffled me off to the synagogue to be part of their choir. The director said I have a very wide range for a male. That just meant I wound up doing lots of solos." He watched her in the large mirror. "I've sung ever since - well, that is until I came up here. I think it was the only thing my father was ever proud that I could do. Everything else was expected - grades in school or winning a case was something I was supposed to do."

"So how did you get into motorcycles?"

"I wanted a dirt bike as a kid. To my dad, it was a fancy toy. He still considers all of it as playing around. He thinks I should grow up, settle down, and be a good lawyer."

Celine turned and wrapped her arms around him. "I like the idea of settling down, but I think it's important that you choose what you truly love doing. And if being president of Tayson and working with Ken Taylor is your passion, then follow it. Do you think I want to work at Crabby's Pot House for the rest of my life?"

"I hope not. I want you to walk in there tomorrow and tell him that you are quitting."

"Guess that means no more flirting with handsome

customers who leave me really big tips along with their phone number."

"Hey, it worked. I only need to hear you say that you'll marry me."

"Yes, I'll marry you. And I'll warn you that, like every little girl who dreams of meeting Prince Charming, I want that wedding with the fancy dress and my dad walking me down the aisle."

"Uh oh. That's not what I had planned."

"What had you planned?"

Celine listened to Frank inhale a deep breath and then say, "I asked Walt Gorman if he'd marry us on Christmas Day. He said he would. Then I planned to take you to see your parents as part of our honeymoon." He grimaced. "How about a compromise? We get married here and you can plan the big church wedding later. I'm sure my family is going to want us married in the synagogue."

"Do I have to turn Jewish?"

He shook his head. "We're rather progressive." Then he grinned at her. "What am I going to have to do to marry you in a church?"

She lifted her shoulder and let it drop. "I feel so stupid. I never thought about the fact that you might be Jewish."

"Does it matter?"

"No, it doesn't. But you don't look Jewish."

"Because my hair isn't dark and my eyes are blue?"

She nodded.

"Am I supposed to be wearing the Star of David on my clothes or walking around with my yarmulke on my head?"

"Oh! That little beanie cap thing, right?"

He chuckled. "Yes. Furthermore, our hearts don't see places of worship, and I really don't think it matters if we have a Christmas tree. I think it looks great, especially with packages under it. I was planning to put a package or two under my tree for you. Am I going to get a present, too?"

She giggled. "Oh, that sounds like a plea for gifts."

He raised his eyebrows. "Would I do that to you?"

She elbowed him. "Are we going back to your cousin's party?"

"Do you want to?"

His question caught her off guard, and what seemed to be a million thoughts flew through her mind. She settled on a few and nodded. "Yes. Want to know why?"

"Okay, I'm game. Why?"

"Because anybody who is anybody in Mariner's Cove is there, and because I've never been to such a party."

"Fine. Shall we go?"

"Let's walk. I know it's cold, but it's so pretty walking through town. And I need to burn off a few calories after that meal."

Frank laughed. "No problem."

They walked up the few blocks to the harbor, and then began their trek around the harbor to the hotel. All the little shops had their windows decorated for Christmas, and there were wreaths on all the doors. The town had decorated the light poles with garland from fir trees, and then wrapped the poles in tiny white lights. And each pole sported a big red ribbon under the light. She stifled her giggle. Each pole was also decorated with a seagull, sitting atop. There were more than enough light poles, but the gulls seemed to enjoy chasing each other. She wondered what they thought of Christmas decorations as she sniffed the air. The scent of the natural greenery mixed with the salt air and had produced a distinctive smell of its own.

Celine wrapped her arm around his waist as they walked in unison. This was home. This was Christmas.

This was the way it should be, she thought, and then wondered what it would be like growing up without Christmas. "Did you get Hanukkah presents?"

"Not exactly, nothing that compared to my gentile friends."

"I can't imagine growing up without Christmas presents, or a Christmas tree, or Christmas songs, or all the other things that go along with Christmas."

"I can see that I will have a lot to learn. Are you willing to learn my religion?"

"Yes."

They passed the parking lot where his car should have been parked instead of in front of her house and continued their walk to the hotel. She pointed to one building. "That's where my father worked for years."

"You said he was a seafood buyer."

"He still is, except now his job is to supervise and train other buyers."

"That's a big company."

"Yes, it is. He probably makes twice the amount of money today than what he made the entire time I was growing up."

"That's probably true for many families, when the children are little and the family seems to need everything, is when parents struggle to make enough money. By the time the children are grown and out of college, that's when the parents have reached a point in their careers when they begin to make decent money. Seems backwards, doesn't it?"

"I'll agree with that."

Some of the boats in the harbor were decorated in Christmas lights. Sailboats had their masts strung with lights and then their owners tied light strings to the fore and aft of the boats as though the lights were sails. Quite a few of the working boats were decorated in wreaths on each side of the bow, and the wreaths decorated the cabins. It seemed as though each owner tried to out-do the other.

"It's beautiful out here tonight. Look at the lights shimmering in the water. And there," she pointed out to sea, "look at the light from the lighthouse as it reflects on the water. Never dreamed I'd see that, not here in Mariner's Cove."

Frank sniffed the icy cold air. "I swear that beacon cost ten times more than it should've. But for Brook and me, it's money well spent. We bought recognition in this community, and that can be priceless. I give Brook another ten or fifteen years, and it wouldn't surprise me to see him run for some major government job. He's a good man and he wants to do what's right."

They walked in silence for a few moments before

Frank spoke again. "Sometimes being a lawyer means that we don't want to ask too many questions. The world isn't black and white. There are a million shades between the two colors."

"Does that mean that you're not happy being a lawyer?"

"I don't mind law, but the way I was forced to handle it... I wanted more. I'm going to like working with Ken, with motorcycles, with riders, and building that business into the next big thing."

"Can you afford to do that? You bought that house and you've done all those renovations. That house will have an outrageous mortgage."

Frank laughed. "Unless I had some sort of drug habit or gambled like crazy, I doubt I could outspend my trust fund." He took a few more steps. "The trick will be to make Tayson a very solvent company. I believe I know how to do that. If I didn't, I wouldn't be taking the job."

"Did you know you're crazy?"

"Yes. Do you realize if you marry me, you'll be marrying crazy?"

"It's crossed my mind." She looked up at him and grinned as they stepped into the hotel. "Let's go have fun."

Celine smiled as she entered the big banquet

room. This was the stuff of childhood dreams, a handsome prince charming, a fabulous dinner, and now the chance to dance the night away. She decided life didn't get better than this.

Whatever problems existed between Brook and Frank seemed to vanish that night. Celine smiled and showed off her ring to the various merchants, the mayor, the chief of emergency services, and quite a few other people she knew from Crabby's. She was no longer the little Colburn kid, or one of Crabby's waitresses. She was about to be Frank's wife for real, and that sent a pulse through her entire system that seemed to quicken her heart and make every step a little lighter. She wanted to call her mom, but she didn't want to break the magic of the evening. Somehow she had become a fairytale princess and the magic was real. Mentally she crossed her fingers, and prayed that it would never end.

The following morning, Celine awoke to the rocking of the yacht. The air was scented with saltwater and coffee. She pointed her toes and lifted her arms over her head, stretching as far as she could. The idea of not having to work was something she could barely comprehend. Her mother had always worked, as had her dad, and from high school forward, she had worked. But if she continued to work… *It would give me my own money.*

"Hi, sleepyhead." He handed her a cup of coffee. "Don't get too spoiled. I will be working again, and I'll be rushing to get out the door, especially if we spend our nights as we did last night."

"Well, maybe I'll be bringing you coffee."

"Oh, I could get into that."

She sat up and tucked the sheet around her. "I need to call my parents and give them the news."

"I called my parents about an hour ago. My dad was thrilled to hear our news. I think he really likes you."

She looked over the rim of her cup and sipped at her coffee. "How about your mom?"

"Relieved. I think she went into a full panic when she discovered that we weren't really married." He shook his head. "I swear if you watched them in court, you'd think they were both icebergs without any emotions. But when it comes to family, they are train wrecks."

"Do they know you are going to work for Ken?"

"I told them, and I'm not just working for Ken, I'm working for myself. I own half that company and probably Ken's soul and first born child."

"I didn't think Ken was married."

"He's not. He can't afford to marry her. And that

first born child is about three months from appearing."

"Oh."

"Could have been worse. Could have been when the racing season was in full swing."

She put her cup down and hurried into the bathroom. When she saw Frank again, she was still on the phone with her mom. She opened the refrigerator door, thinking she'd fix breakfast, but the shelves were empty.

Frank grinned. "Guess if we want to eat, I'll have to take you to the hotel. I hope you are hungry."

"Starved." She held one finger up in the air. "Am I going to have to live my life around motocross races?"

After breakfast, Frank took her on his cycle to meet Ken and see where they were building the motorcycles. To watch the excitement in her eyes told him that she would fit right in with his friends. Then they went into the city to have a late dinner with Ken and his girlfriend. The whole day had been exceptional and the ride home was clear. They stopped once just to see all the stars.

"Here." She handed him her phone. "It's an app. Point the phone at the stars."

"Oh, this is amazing."

They got back on the cycle and continued towards Mariner's Cove. As they approached, Frank asked, "Your place or mine?"

"Mine. I need some things."

The next morning, Frank awakened to an empty bed. He found a note on the kitchen table saying she had a few errands and to make himself at home. He looked at the clock and realized he hadn't slept that late since he'd been a teen. He scribbled under her note. "ME, TOO!"

A few minutes later, he was at his new house. Nothing remained of the old house except for some exterior work that would be done in the spring. The old walls were gone. He had virtually flipped the house. Now the living areas all faced the water, including the master bedroom. Everything was new. When he thought of the previous owner, his skin crawled. The house had been erased of all resemblance to its former owner. He wanted a fresh look with clean lines, but he had the feeling that Celine would want to choose the furniture.

The general contractor, Mike Silvia, came around

the corner. "Didn't hear you come in."

"Just wanted to see how far along you were."

"Close to finishing up."

"It looks better than I thought it would."

"I'll take that as a compliment."

"Yeah, it is." He pointed to a few steel posts. "What about those?"

"When you know your style, I'll match it."

Frank knew he was dependent on the contractor, as he knew nothing about buildings. But the residents in Mariner's Cove were decent honest people and he liked that. He also liked the fact that Celine seemed to know everyone.

He wandered into what would be their bedroom. Sun would fill this room most of the day, and the way it faced, they would get plenty of breeze. He looked out the side before opening the door and stepping onto a patio for a moment. He envisioned a private area just for them with a hot tub - a romantic area where they could frolic and play. Cold air sent him back inside.

He looked out the glass wall into the backyard and across to the ocean. When he leaned down and put his hands on his knees, the ocean vanished. He wanted to see that ocean from his bed.

"Hey, Mike?" Frank called.

"Got a question?"

"Yeah, what would it take to raise the floor so I can look at the ocean from the bed?"

The contractor grimaced. "Buy the bed. Then we can figure it out. Probably a simple platform."

"Loft?"

"It's your money."

Frank had more to do than to stand around daydreaming.

Chapter 8

*C*eline wanted something special to wear for her marriage to Frank. She remembered seeing it when she had been looking for some jewelry to wear to Brook's party. It wasn't particularly dressy or fancy, but it was the sort of thing that she could wear again. Made in two pieces, the ensemble consisted of a simple dress and a wool coat in a winter white. She paid for the outfit and left the mall.

Her mind swirled with thoughts. She wasn't some childish waif who'd been swept off her feet. She was a grown woman who had dated plenty of men and never found anyone who could compare to Frank.

Her medical-laboratory billing job accepted her plea for time off and so did Crabby. Then she wondered what she would do. She realized she almost envied Nikki because she worked every day with her husband. Celine knew she didn't want to rely on Frank for money. She wanted her own, but she had time to decide.

She thought about the Christmas gifts that she had bought Frank and knew he'd be thrilled.

She stopped by the docks and realized his cycle was gone. Bobby Finch held the gate open for her and she tucked her gifts under his Christmas tree, except for one. She had to enlist the help of one of the watermen she knew to get the chimenea from the trunk of her car to the yacht.

She parked the outdoor fireplace near the tree, and stacked the small bag of charcoal on top of it. Then she took a roll of wrapping paper and managed to get it covered before Frank came home and found it.

She couldn't imagine what it must have been like growing up Jewish, but she knew she would learn. She also knew she wasn't about to give up her own beliefs.

This would be their first Christmas together and the day they were married. She believed things happened for a reason. If she had left with her parents, she would have never worked at Crabby's and never meet Frank.

Two days later, she stood on the deck of Frank's yacht with Brook and Nikki, Lisa and her boyfriend, Andy and his friend, and Crabby and his wife in attendance as Walt Gorham married Celine and Frank.

Mixed thoughts flowed through Celine as Frank placed the diamond-studded wedding band on her finger. Now she was married for real. She wasn't certain how she'd gotten so lucky. She looked into Frank's face and fought with the tears of joy. But the bliss came with a price. Her life would circulate around a racing schedule. She wouldn't be married in the church for several months, did that still make her married in God's eyes? And what would it be like to be married in a synagogue? Now she'd be part of his large crazy family. Would she be able to stay out of the family fracas, or would she be pulled back into it? *I only want to be with Frank.*

When the ceremony was over, he threaded her fingers with his as they all walked to the hotel for an early dinner. No matter what life held in store for them, she knew they would face it together. Nothing would keep them apart. He squeezed her hand as though he'd been reading her mind.

Her prince charming wasn't an ordinary man - he

looked at challenges, broke them into pieces, and devoured them. He was fearless, and his armor was a motorcycle.

Fini

The Charity Auction

*E*lke pulled her coat a little tighter over her costume as she entered the big room. *Oh was this a mistake!* She handed over her invitation to the Riverside University Children's Hospital Christmas Auction, as her gut clenched tighter. *Why did I let my friends talk me into this?* From fairy princesses to creatures from outer space, the costumes were spectacular. Hers was cobbled together from a thrift store find.

She thought she had struck gold when she found a black leotard, tights, and a pair of ballet slippers. She'd pulled the strings on those slippers and tightened the elastic that went across her instep to make them tight enough to stay on her feet. She hadn't had ballet since she was a teen, but she loved it. With her hair pulled into a bun at the nape of her neck and the black slip that she remade into a ballet skirt, she thought she looked like a black swan. She'd taken extra care with her dramatic eye makeup, pulled on her coat, and left her apartment feeling very good about the evening.

Right now, as she looked around the room, she wanted to hide in a corner and vanish from sight. There was even another black swan, but she was done up in feathers, looking fabulous.

Elke handed over her coat as a woman dressed like Marie Antoinette was placing a numbered band on her arm. "What *are* you?"

Elke forced a grin. "The ugly duckling."

"Good luck, honey. You're going to need it."

Elke spotted Brittany, who was dressed like Morticia, except the dress was cut much lower.

"Elke!" another voice called.

Elke turned and saw a green elf rushing towards her. It was her friend Joanne, complete with pointed ears and enough sequins to make Liberace look paltry.

"What do you think of my new haircut?" the elf asked when she came to a halt.

"And you dyed your hair green?"

"No, that's just green hair spray. But isn't my cut adorable? I just love it!"

"Okay, the green washes out, and that's not a wig?"

Joanne reached up and tugged at her bangs. "Nope, mine."

"Cute, definitely cute. Very different. Um, it gives you a whole new look." *What was she thinking?*

"Yes, different. That's what I thought. Makes my eyes look bigger."

By then, 'Morticia' had joined them. "What *are* you?"

"The ugly duckling."

"I told you to wear something sexy and beautiful. How are you supposed to attract a man looking like that?"

Elke rolled her eyes. "At a Christmas charity auction? Come on, really? What guy is seriously on the make at something like this? And would I want someone who is?"

"'Elk', half these guys are residents at the hospital, or young doctors just getting started. I promise at least half are on the make." Brittany crossed her arms over her ample chest that needed a little more coverage.

"Lighten up." Joanne, the sequined elf, demanded as she grabbed Elke's arm and looked at the number printed on her wristband. "Omigod, you're number nine! The bidding is heavy in the beginning. I've heard that several doctors have pledged bids of at least twenty-five thousand dollars." Joanne twirled and waved her star wand. "I'm fifty-six."

"I'm a hundred and thirteen. Wouldn't it have been a hoot if I were thirteen? But no, I have to get the hundred in front of it." Brittany ran her fingers through her long black wig. "I bought it online. I should get someone's attention in this costume. Don't you think?"

Jack the Ripper? "Isn't it cut a wee bit low?" Elke asked.

"Nothing shows; it's just cleavage. Stop being a prude."

That's a whole lot more than cleavage.

Joanne pressed her palm to her forehead. "This room is way too hot! My green makeup will be running to my knees."

"Ladies, the bidding will start in forty-five minutes. Please keep your voices to a whisper." Marie Antoinette demanded.

The two friends wandered off to chat with another friend and that gave Elke the break she needed. She wasn't certain if it was the heat in the room, the cloying scent of heavy perfumes, or her nerves, but she needed fresh air before she passed out. Trying a side door, it opened onto a patio. *Thank goodness!* Using her toes, she dropped the stopper on the bottom of the door and the stopper caught on the pavement about four inches before the door closed. She ran her fingertips over her forehead and prayed she didn't break out into a full sweat. Her breath in the cold air floated in front of her face like a small cloud.

It's a silly auction. I'm doing my part in this moneymaker for the children's hospital. I just have to get through the night with some guy who has onion breath and has paid a few bucks to have dinner with me. What if no one bids on me?

The memory of her last dance recital drifted through her mind. Then her parent's divorce put an end to her dance lessons. Her mom couldn't afford them.

Elke jumped and criss-crossed her feet a few times before landing. Doing something felt good. A few *glissades*, another *entrechat*, and some confidence filtered back into her. She missed ballet. *Maybe I should take some adult classes just for the exercise?* Lost in dance, she realized she was not alone when she heard clapping.

"Bravo!" Not more than twenty feet away, tucked into the darkness, stood a shadowy figure of a man leaning against the building.

She peered into the darkness. "Aren't you supposed to be inside getting ready for the big auction, or do you work for the hotel?"

He leaned forward and balanced on his feet. "I'm supposed to be inside. Let's leave it with I'm hiding. And why aren't you inside?"

"It's blazing hot in there. I couldn't breathe."

"So what are you supposed to be, a music box dancer?"

Elke giggled. "Then I'd need a pink tutu, and I'd have to do *pirouettes*. I was trying to look like the black swan, but..." She forced a smile. "But discovered I'm the ugly duckling."

"Why do you say that?"

"Wait 'til you see the costumes."

"This must be your first time."

She nodded as she sat on the stone bench and faced the man's voice, wishing she could see his face. "Friends talked me into it. I figured it was for the kids, and well... I'd do anything to help them and their families. I mean, this is a way for me to...you know...give back."

"Who are your friends?"

"Brittany Hughes, she's a drug rep. And Joanne Bloxom, she's Dr. Tansy's patient liaison."

"Dr. Tansy is an excellent surgeon."

"You know him?"

"Yeah, you could say that." He jerked his thumb over his shoulder. "Marie Antoinette is his wife."

"Really? Wow. I had no idea."

"Yeah, she pours her heart and soul into this auction. It's a family thing."

"So you know her?"

"She's been recruiting me to help her for years." He leaned back against the wall.

Elke didn't like talking to a shadow, but he posed no threat.

"Are you a real ballerina?"

"No. I took lessons as a kid. But I was going to be far too tall to seriously consider doing anything with it. But I've always loved it. I'd kill to see a real performance." She rubbed her arms that were now feeling the cold air.

Brittany stuck her nose out the door. "There you are. Get in here. We're lining up."

"Got to run. Nice chatting with you. I think my butterflies have settled down." Elke raised her hand in a wave. "Wish me luck." She stopped for moment.

"I just hope someone nice bids on me. It's a little like being in elementary school and hoping you're not the last person chosen for the team."

A woman checked the wristbands against a list and put everyone in numeric order. Slowly the women being auctioned moved closer to the door where the auction took place. Wonder Woman was number eight, and she filled out the costume probably better than Lynda Carter.

"Dr. Rosalind Deerfield, one of Children's Hospital's residents is number eight. She likes watching ice hockey, and enjoys hitting the slopes in the winter."

The crowd cheered and clapped loudly.

Elke felt the hand on her back pushing her out the door. She walked up the two steps onto the platform and stood in the center.

"Um, Forgive me, everyone, I've lost my place." Marie Antoinette turned from the mike. "You're number nine? I don't seem to have your name."

Elke did a gracious curtsy and went to Marie Antoinette. "Elke Dersmouth. I'm the outpatient-scheduling clerk at the hospital."

"Thank you, darling." The woman turned back to the mike and gave everyone Elke's name.

Elke walked away with only the sounds of rustling

papers and some polite clapping. She wanted to crawl into a mouse hole and never come out. Instead, she ran to the ladies room and hid in a stall until she could compose herself. If she bolted out the door... *Who would know? I would. I'm doing this for the kids.* All she could do was cross her fingers.

"Elk', are you in here?" Brittany called.

"Yes. I'm hiding."

"What went wrong out there?"

"I have no clue." *Story of my life.*

"Let's get a glass of wine while we wait."

⁕

Kevin Tansy placed his bid in the envelope and turned it in. There was no way he was going to allow anyone to outbid him. He stepped into the dining room and into a gaggle of anxious women.

Rosalind Deerfield immediately sashayed to his side. "I do hope you weren't outbid."

"So do I." He searched the room.

"I have champagne waiting for us at my place." She ran her hand up his arm. "We'll make it a memorable night."

In your dreams, Roz. "I'm certain it will be

unforgettable."

"Kevin, Kevin!"

Inwardly he groaned, as several women approached him. He lifted his phone from its clip, "Excuse me, ladies."

He stepped into the hotel's lobby, then outside. Knowing approximately how long it would take to tally the bids, gave him a slight advantage, because he had no intention of staying for the catered dinner. He'd take her to a quiet restaurant. At the moment, he was thankful that he wasn't the one being auctioned.

*

Marie Antoinette took the microphone. "Ladies and gentlemen. Thank you all for being part of this Christmas event. We've had an extremely successful evening. Tonight's highest bidder is Dr. Weiner... Oh, wait. My mistake. The highest bidder tonight is..." Again, she conferred with someone then glared at her son as though he'd lost his mind. "The highest bidder is Dr. Kevin Tansy with thirty-six thousand dollars--"

The crowd roared.

Brittany tugged her dress and wiggled a little. Elke

rolled her eyes and Joanne laughed.

Marie Antoinette held up her hands until the room quieted. "Kevin's date for tonight is Elke Dersmouth, our sweet little ballerina."

Joanne's fist intersected Elke's upper arm. "Who did you bribe?"

"Huh?"

"She called your name."

"What? Me? No way. Someone hit the wrong box on the list. They need to check that again. They probably wanted Wonder Woman."

"Elk'!" Brittany pushed Elke forward and called, "She's in shock."

The room broke into giggles and then started clapping.

Dr. Kevin Tansy was waiting for her on the mini platform.

"I'm sorry, there must be a mistake," Elke babbled, as she stepped into the poinsettia-decorated rostrum to greet the handsome man.

He smiled at her and held out his hand.

Elke took the proffered hand, but could feel the heat flowing over her cheeks. She smiled and waved. With her teeth clenched, she said, "I'm sorry, it's a mistake, right? I understand."

He leaned over and whispered in her ear. "I don't

make thirty-six thousand dollar mistakes." Without letting go of her hand, he put his other hand on her back and led her from the room. "We'll get your coat. I guarantee you don't want the stuffed chicken breast."

"I don't understand."

"I promise, I'm very nice. I actually love watching the ballet, and no one ever wants to be the last person chosen for the team."

Fini

DID YOU ENJOY READING
BABY, IT'S COLD OUTSIDE **BY E. AYERS?**

Please leave a short review on your favorite venue and let your book retailer know how much you enjoyed it! Independent authors count on your reviews to help them succeed.

You can write to the author directly at the following website: www.ayersbooks.com

About the Author

Born and raised with wealth, E. Ayers turned away from all of it and married a few days after turning eighteen, to the shock and dismay of family and friends.

A firm believer in love conquering everything, there was never cause to look back. The newlyweds' life-long love became the springboard for many future novels.

Fascinated with the way people deal with everyday problems, E. Ayers has always been an observer and a listener. A simple problem for one person is a mountain for another. Utilizing those common predicaments, the subsequent novels have touched many lives.

Today finds E. Ayers writing while living in a pre-Civil War home with a dog and a cat. Rattling around in an old money pit provides one's muse with plenty of freedom. A perfect day is spent at the keyboard, coffee in hand, and everything in the house actually working as it should.

As the official matchmaker for all the characters who wander through a mind full of imagination and the need to share, E. Ayers enjoys finding just the right ones to create a story.

More Great Books From E. Ayers

About the Publisher

Indie Artist Press is a hybrid publisher, which mean that the quality books you find in our catalogue are written by independent authors who earn 100% of the proceeds from their work while they invest in their own literary futures.

At IAP, we believe that there are many, many incredibly talented authors out there who deserve to maintain this type of control over their product. We also believe that you, the reader, deserve the highest quality books to satisfy your discriminating taste.

We hand select each book we include in our catalogue with a rigorous submission process that ensures you will receive a book worth reading every time.

To find more excellent examples of indie books, please visit our website at www.indieartistpress.com.